STOP!

Wait, actually, don't stop—read every word (preferably twice) and tell all your friends how much you loved *The Savage Gentleman*!

. . . And make sure you check out the free sneak peak of the first two chapters of my upcoming sexy HEA rom-com, ***The Three Kiss Clause***, coming December 2019.

You can read right at the end of this book.

And remember to add to your Goodreads TBR here—> https://www.goodreads.com/book/ show/47566019-the-three-kiss-clause

Happy reading!

Cover
Coming
Soon

SYNOPSIS

My name is Lucas "The Ghost" Esparza.

I'm the best MMA fighter in the world that you've never heard of, but if I have my way, I'll be a household name soon enough. My life's been nothing but hard training, crazy partying, and fast women, and that's just how I liked it. No man had ever gotten the better of me inside the cage, and no woman had ever been able to slow down my lifestyle outside of it.

And then it all came crashing down.

When I tasted defeat for the first time in the biggest fight of my life, I was a broken man—my pride destroyed and my dreams of greatness deferred.

That's when Mila walked into my gym.

When my trainer told me I had to giver her self defense lessons because she was a 'special case', I had no idea what he meant. All I knew was that she had a body to die for, and a face that made me forget my own name. I'd been with my share of women, but she was easily the sexiest I'd ever laid eyes on.

There was only one problem—we hated each other with a passion!

I thought she was whiny with a bad attitude. She thought I was full of myself. But then something happened that changed everything between us. She gave me the confidence to pursue my dreams once again—to be a champion, to make it into the UFC, and to be the savage gentleman that I was born to be.

PROLOGUE

MILA

The canvas beneath my feet has an unexpected bounce to it—a give that makes me feel like a little kid jumping up and down on a bed. It causes me to lose my balance for a second. I go to grab the ropes to keep from falling, but, before I can, he clasps onto my arm. His grasp is strong, and it keeps me stable. His touch wakes my body from a slumber I didn't realize it was in, and when he lets go of me I miss the warmth of his skin.

He's standing behind me now, and his hands have gone from support to something else. His fingers are clutching my hips, holding me in place. I don't move and I don't resist. I stand still, waiting to see what he's going to do next. He positions himself behind me, and I feel the heat of his body against my back.

The peach fuzz on the back of my neck stands up, and a

warm sensation runs the length of my body. He has this effect on me. He's the only one who's ever made me feel this way.

He doesn't know about my past yet. He doesn't know the awful situation I'm coming from, or the damage that it did to me. But when I'm with him, I forget all of that—as if it never happened, and I let my body do the thinking for me. I lean back, gently, and press into the hardness of his body, and I feel a fire between my legs.

I didn't come here expecting this, but almost everything that's happened with him has been unexpected.

Lucas "The Ghost" Esparza.

My savage gentleman.

ONE YEAR AGO

Lucas

The blood reminds me that I'm alive.

For a normal person, blood signifies that something's gone wrong, but for a guy like me, it means that the party's just getting started.

The lights are blinding. The cheer of the crowd is nothing short of deafening. That's how it should be. We put our health—even our lives—on the line for other people's entertainment, the least they can do is scream for us as though we were the gladiators of the Roman Empire.

I breathe in as deeply as my lungs will allow, and that oxygen is going to sustain me through the next few seconds. In that time, I'll rush towards my opponent and he'll rush towards me.

Our fists will be up, our mouthpieces will be bitten down on, and then we'll engage in the last acceptable act of war in our society. It's an environment I thrive in.

In this cage, I know who I am, who I want to be, and the difference between the two. There's nothing in here but the purest form of honesty, and no illusions are allowed.

That's just the way I like it.

There are few human beings on this earth who can do what I do, and even fewer who want to.

I'm a modern-day warrior, and inside the octagon is where I call home.

CHAPTER ONE

LUCAS

I'm a bad motherfucker.

The sooner we get that fact out there, the better.

But let the stereotypes go. I don't come from the mean streets of. . . *wherever*—I grew up a suburban boy—I went to a Catholic school that cost my parents six thousand dollars a year, and I played baseball on Saturday afternoons with my friends. I finished high school with a decent GPA, and then got my undergrad degree at the local university. I'm normal kid from a middle class home—the guy next door—except for one thing.

I fuck people up inside a cage for a living.

I guess saying that I'm normal is a little misleading. Better to say that I *grew up* normal, but I have a different mindset than most people. I didn't start fighting because I had no other options in life, or because I was trying to work my way out of poverty. I fight for two reasons—one, I have a bad temper that demands satisfaction, and two, I have a burning desire to prove that I'm the best there is at this game.

Now, before we go any further, let me ask you a few questions—when was the last time you got punched in the face? How about the last time you got leg kicked so hard your body fell over? Or maybe you can tell me all about the last time you got choked out and had to tap your hands on another person's body to make them stop before you passed out from a lack of blood to the brain?

I'm guessing that for most of you the answer to all these questions is a resounding 'never'. But for me, those question don't even apply. The right question to ask someone like me isn't how many times I've gotten hit, its how many times did the other guy miss, and how many times did I hit him back?

And the answer to both—*a fucking lot.*

I'm a professional fighter—Lucas "The Ghost" Esparza —maybe you've seen some of my fights on YouTube. Probably you haven't. I'm not a famous fighter just yet, but if I have my way tonight, I won't ever have to introduce myself to you again. You know Conor McGregor? Ronda Rousey? Jon Jones? Of course you do, everyone does.

They're crossover successes—fighters with multiple world championships, TV deals, endorsements, and more money than they could spend in a lifetime. One day I'll be a household name like they are, but for right now I'm just a hungry kid working his way up the ladder of the local New York amateur circuit, trying to get himself into the show of shows—the Ultimate Fighting Championships—which you probably know better as the UFC.

I might be giving you the wrong impression. I'm not a violent man, per say, but I do have violence in me. Who knows where that comes from. That's one of the many stereotypes that exist about men like me: that we're sociopaths, that we like to hurt people, that we come from abusive homes where we were taught how to be aggressive. Bullshit. Just plain bullshit. But I don't blame people for thinking that. A lot of it comes from where the sport started.

MMA was banned in most states when it first appeared on people's radar in the early 1990's. Back then there were no rules. You could literally stomp on a guy's face while he was on the ground, elbow someone to the back of the head, and do almost anything else, except eye gouging and biting. It was a circus back in the day—there were no weight classes, everyone (and I mean everyone) was on steroids, and calling it a sport would be a giant misnomer. Senator John McCain famously called it 'human cock fighting', and helped to get it banned in most states.

The first images everyone had of mixed martial arts was the spectacle of different sized men brawling like they would in a bar—and you know what they say about first impressions. Those days were crazy, but that's not how things are anymore. Today the sport is an actual *sport*—legal in all fifty states, regulated by state athletic commissions with rules and regulations, and is currently one of the most popular sports in the United States.

But stereotypes die hard, and a lot of people still hold them about both the sport and the athletes themselves. When I tell people what I do for a living they look at me sideways—like I might be a threat to them, like I'm a psycho, like I might throw them down and try to break one of their limbs. But, like I said, I'm not a violent guy. There are too many differences between professional fighters and violent people to even list, but one of the biggest ones is that fighters have a context to their violence—a switch that they can turn on or off so that they can express their violence in an agreed upon contest.

Take me for example. As soon as a contract is signed and my money is guaranteed, I'll fight any man on this planet. Once me and that other man agree to throw down and test our skills against one another, it's on. I abandon the normal part of me—the one with sympathy and emotions, and I replace it with the version of myself that's necessary to fight another man in a cage. And then, when the contest is over, I'm back to being me. My opponent and I shake hands, hug, tell each other 'good fight', and our corners—our coaches and trainers— shake hands with one other.

Inside that octagon I have no fear, no guilt, no conscience, and I pray that my opponent doesn't either. I don't want his mercy, or his concern for my well being—I only want to test myself using one simple question: can my violence defeat his? If the answer is yes, then I'm the man—the alpha—the badass motherfucker who no one can touch. And if the answer is no, then I don't deserve any of this—not the fame I seek, or the recognition I want, or the women who always hang around the sport.

The women. Let's stop and talk about them for a minute.

No matter how many women tell you they don't like fighting, what they do love is a man who can fight. Sure, some women are into the sport, but most aren't. It's a rare woman who'll sit down ringside where you can practically feel the beads of sweat and blood hitting you. But what they really like—even the ones who pretend not to—is a man like me. An alpha. A badass. A guy who can kick the shit out of their man without breaking a sweat. A man like me has no trouble meeting women, and the more I win inside that octagon, the easier it gets to meet them. And I win—a lot.

My dream, like all fighters, is to make it to the UFC—an organization that has so much name recognition that now everyone in the country knows what it is. It's such a monolith that people say UFC when they mean MMA. More than one woman has asked me—*so you do that UFC stuff?* Of course, I nod and say yes because that shit is a panty dropper, but the truth is I haven't made it to the big stage yet. It's my dream—why I train, why I sacrifice, why I get my ass kicked in order to get better.

That's why tonight's fight means everything.

I don't like to hype my fights up too much, but there's a special guest sitting in the audience tonight, and if you knew who he was, you'd understand why I'm more nervous than usual for this fight. My coach called me into his office at our gym a few days ago to break the news to me.

"Lucas, get in here when you're done with your roll."

"Yes, sir."

I was just playing with my training partner—letting him think he had the better of me before I reversed the position and submitted him in seconds. After he tapped out, I jumped up and went into the back.

"What is it, Master Splinter?"

"Are you ever going to get tired of calling me that?" he asked.

"No, sir. Only when I become a master myself. Then I guess we'll both be masters, so I'll just call you Splinter."

"You can just call me Matt. You know, since it's my name and all."

"Sure, I could," I joked, "but what fun would that be?"

"My name doesn't have to be fun, you know?"

"So, what's going on Master Splinter Matt?"

"You can be such a huge dick sometimes, you know that?"

"If you weren't my coach this would be the part where I told you 'that's what she said.'"

Matt's a cool guy—old school in some ways, like when it comes to basic student-teacher respect, but still a cool, relatively young guy in his mid forties.

"And if you weren't my student, that would be the part where I died laughing. I didn't even realize when I said it."

"I know," I tell him. "That's why it was funny."

Matt broke character for a few seconds and laughs hysterically with me.

"So, what did you need, Coach?"

"Ah, so we're back to being serious about your career? Good."

"My career?" I asked.

"Look, the last thing I want to do is put more pressure on you for Saturday's fight. But this is kind of like when you're a chef and there's a critic for the New York Times coming to your restaurant for dinner. Know what I'm referring to?"

"No way. You don't mean?"

"Uh-huh."

My mouth hung open. "Sean is going to be there?"

"The one and only."

Sean Graham is the matchmaker and talent scout for the UFC. He's the gatekeeper of dreams, the man who makes all of the decisions for who goes onto the big show and who doesn't. Sean is known for going around to local organizations and looking for talent to sign. If you're good—and especially if you're a champion in a smaller division, your chances of getting in are all but guaranteed. My organization, New York Cage Fighting Championships, has had three guys in as many years get into the UFC. One of them, Kane Koz, made a run for the lightweight championship last year and lost by a razor thin decision. He was our 'Rocky' story—his poster still hangs in the back locker room.

Right now, I'm the number one contender in my division—light heavyweight, which is 205 pounds—which means that if I win tonight, I'm a champion, and the odds of getting a backstage visit from Sean go up exponentially. And if I have a spectacular performance—like a knockout or submission finish—he might even offer me a UFC contract on the spot.

Now I'm backstage, warming up in the dressing room as the co-main event fight is going down. I passively watch it on the TV as I do some light sparring and Jiu Jitsu drills, and the roars of the crowd builds my anticipation of getting out there myself and having the performance of a lifetime.

A submission—a rear naked choke—ends the fight, and that only means one thing.

It's five minutes until I'm up.

I do a few drills to pass the time, so I don't have to think about how nervous I am, and I keep my sweat up so I'm not cold when I get out there. By the time my muscles are warm and ready to put a hurting on the guy across from me in the cage, I get the call.

"You're up, Lucas."

My music starts playing—Rage Against the Machine's *Killing in the Name*—and I walk to the octagon, my team behind me. I've never been so nervous for a fight. I don't feel like myself. Normally I'm cocky—sure of myself—ready to beat the guy across from me to a bloody pulp, but I'm not feeling that right now. I'm not feeling like 'The Ghost' — I'm feeling something I haven't felt in a long time—like I'm out of my league.

What makes this match even more exciting is the fact that we're both undefeated. My opponent—the light heavyweight champion of the New York Cage Fight Championships, Wes Finley, has an undefeated record of 9–0, and I have a record of 11–0. They titled tonight's event 'Someone's O has to go!' I plan on being Wes' first defeat, but as I see him walking to the cage my heart is in my throat.

Our names are announced, and the fight begins. . .

CHAPTER TWO

LUCAS

Ten Minutes Later

What happened? Where am I?

I open up my eyes, and the lights from the doctor's little flashlight are shining so brightly that my impulse is to close them again. My team is standing over me, and the noise is deafening.

They lift me up on a stool and I sit, disoriented, looking around. The crowd is going nuts, and Wes is running around the octagon with his hands up and hugging his team. He comes up to me, as I try to balance on my stool, and leans in. "Good fight, bro. You're a tough kid, you'll be a champion one day."

My head is so fucked up that I can't really understand what's happening, but I understand the only part that matters—I lost.

I didn't just lose a fight. I lost an opportunity that I may never get back.

A little while later, with my senses coming back to me, I

sit in the locker room with only Matt, my striking coach Al, and my wounded ego.

"What was it?" I ask.

"Left high kick. It was sneaky. He threw a punch first to get your hands blocking your right side, then he threw high to your left."

There's an old expression in fighting—*the most dangerous strike is the one that you don't see coming*. I didn't even know what hit me. I had to wake up and be told by my team. This is the most unforgiving sport there is.

Wes comes by my dressing room one more time to basically say the same thing he'd said in the octagon after he'd knocked me out cold. He's got the championship belt slung over his shoulder, and he doesn't even look like he's been in much of a fight. He looks like he just had a hard cardio day at the gym. *Fuck*. He comes over and hugs me again.

"You're a great fighter man, don't be disappointed. You'll be back."

I want to hate the guy who just slammed his giant shin into the side of my head and cost me my dream, but there are two reasons I can't—one, Wes is a super nice guy despite the fact that he looks like a character from Mad Max. And two, this is the fight game. Sometimes you're the hammer, and other times you're just the fucking nail.

As I get up to shower, get dressed, and get the hell out of there—with my ego bruised and my heart broken, I see Sean Graham standing by the locker room door with a bunch of suits. I recognize him immediately, only he's not here for me.

"Wes!" he shouts. "Come on, we have some business to discuss."

Yeah. I know exactly what that *business* is. That should

be me walking over to Sean right now. That's how it was supposed to go. That's how I visualized it. And that's exactly what didn't happen. This really is the hurting game.

As I turn my back, I hear Sean's voice one more time, and this time it is for me.

"Lucas," he says. I turn around. "You were doing well until you got caught. It happens. You're an exciting fighter. Keep at it, alright?"

"Thanks, Sean. Thanks for coming out."

Those aren't the words I was meant to say to him. I was meant to say . . . *of course I'll sign the contract to fight in the UFC. I'm so happy! I won't let you guys down!*

The universe had other plans for me.

Oh, well. Back to the drawing board we go.

Time to climb back up the ladder.

CHAPTER THREE

MILA

I struggle to open my eyes, and when I try, only one does what I want it to do.

The other eye—the one I'm trying to open— is sealed completely shut. I hear a beeping around me, and I can't move my body to do much except blink. My eyelid will still listen to me, but the rest of my body isn't responding. When my one good eyelid lifts up, I see my family standing over me. My mom is holding my hand, and my dad is standing near my feet, looking upset. I hear them calling my name, and my brother yells for a doctor or nurse to come into the room because I'm awake.

I'm confused at first, and when I try to talk it's a struggle. It's like my brain knows what I'm trying to say, but my ears hear a jumbled mess of sounds. I try again and the same thing happens. I start to get upset and try to move my body around but I can't. That's when I really start to panic.

My mom puts her hand on my shoulder to comfort me. It doesn't work. That's when I hear her voice in my ear.

"Stay still, baby. You're okay. You're at the hospital.

Something happened and you were hurt. Don't be afraid, the doctors are working to make you all better."

The doctors come in and try to soothe me also. A bunch of nurses flood the room. The beeping of my machine gets louder, and that makes me panic. I try to move for a second time but nothing happens at all.

My mom is still talking to me, trying to tell me everything will be okay, but I know something bad happened and nothing will be okay again. Adrenaline is coursing through my body as I try to get it to respond to me.

I don't see it happen, but they must have given me something to calm me down. My eyelid—the only part of my body that I can control, starts to close. As it does, I feel nothing but fear, but soon that's replaced by total blackness.

CHAPTER FOUR

PRESENT DAY

FOUR

Lucas

My coach, Matt, says that staying humble is everything.
I'm not so good with humility.

There are a few ways that coaches can help with that.
Really old school coaches—which luckily Matt is not—
would have beaten you down—literally—or had other guys
in the gym work you over until both your body and your ego
were bruised up nicely, and you'd learned your place in the
pecking order. No one trains like that anymore. Instead,
Matt keeps my ego in check by having me teach privates
and classes.

Even though I can teach all of the disciplines, mostly I
teach Jiu Jitsu, which is a grappling and submission art. It's
one of the four main disciplines used in MMA, along with
boxing, Muay Thai and wrestling. Jiu Jitsu is called the
'gentle art' because you can win a match with a submission,
and your opponent can tap out to end the fight. Not all
sports are like that—there's no giving up in boxing. You just
keep getting hit until the fight is over. Because Jiu Jitsu

teaches discipline, body control, and is the best martial art for self-defense, there are kids classes offered all the time.

The truth is I really love the kids that I work with, and they love training with a real-life MMA fighter. I have a class of three boys and six girls, and even though I protested for a long time when Matt asked—forget that, when Matt *told* me that I was teaching—I love helping the kids build up their confidence and self defense skills.

But, at first, my ego was too big—I admit it now. It was a year and a half ago. I'd just won three fights in a short time, all by knockout or submission. My head was too big to even fit through the door, and Wes hadn't knocked me back down to earth. At the time I thought I was better than all my team mates, thought I knew more than my head coach (who knows almost everything about the game), and I definitely thought that I was too good to teach some kids' class. I remember how the conversation went with Matt.

"Get James to do it," I'd said defiantly. "I don't want to teach. I'm a fighter, not a coach."

"James is busy."

"Busy? Busy doing what? He doesn't even have a fight coming up!"

I heard the arrogance in my voice when I asked the question, but I wasn't capable of not sounding that way. Matt looked up and took his glasses off.

"It doesn't matter what," he said. "I'm telling you that I need you to do this, so asking me if someone else can do it sounds like you're trying to ignore your responsibility."

"Responsibility? To who? I didn't sign up to teach some stupid classes."

"Your responsibility it to this gym—to me, and all of your other coaches who give you a platform to train and get where you want to get. We put hours into you and your career, that we don't charge you for. Hours spent watching film of your opponents, phone calls to each other to strategize for your upcoming fight, and a million other things you don't see. We do that for you, because it's our job to make you better. But you owe it to give back to the gym that's given to you, to help the next line of future champions, or whoever walks through those front doors to learn. You understand me?"

Matt has a way of putting me in my place that doesn't make me want to fight him. He's probably the only man on earth who has that capability. I've never gotten along with authority figures—I got suspended in my freshman year of high school for stupid stuff like 'insubordination', which is basically a nice way of saying I acted like a dick to my teachers. The next year is when my parents finally had enough and took me to the gym as a last-ditch effort. So, I met Matt when I was a sophomore—fifteen years old —and almost got kicked out of school for some serious stuff.

My parents didn't know what to do with me, and even though we got along, they just couldn't get through to me, so instead they tried something that turned out to be the best decision of my life—they brought me to my first martial arts class. That's when I met Matt, and that's when I learned how to respect authority figures.

Matt kicked my butt into shape—made clay into something resembling a statue—but it took some time. I'm a stubborn man, and I was even worse at fifteen, but Matt found a way to break through when he asked me a very specific question. To this day I have no idea how he even knew to ask me. This is why I call him 'Splinter', like Master Splinter from Teenaged Mutant Ninja Turtles—the old wise rat who always knows how to say the right thing.

"Lucas, I want to ask you something, and you don't have to tell me the answer if you don't want to, alright?"

"What is it?" I ask, scared as to what this guy I barely knew at the time was going to ask.

"Have you ever been bullied?"

It was like he was seeing into my life, seeing something that I never told anyone, not even my mom and dad. I was so freaked out by the question that I didn't say anything. I looked at him like an idiot, my mouth hanging open like I was going to say something, only nothing would come out. All that time, Matt just kept looking into my eyes, asking the question again without actually asking it again out loud. He just waited, patiently, until I finally answered. Well, sort of answered.

"How... how did you know?"

"Because I've been doing this for a long time, and I've seen what happens when kids get bullied."

"What do you mean 'what happens'?"

I'll never forget what he said to me next. "Insecurities. You're filled with them. I can see it all over you, from how you carry yourself, to how you behave, to how your parents tell me you behave at school. You're an insecure young man."

I'd never heard anyone say anything like that to me. No one ever suggested anything so preposterous to my fifteen-year-old mind. Like most things I wasn't comfortable with back then, I just rejected it outright.

"Insecure? Me? Are you nuts?"

"I'm not nuts, and when you talk to me I need you to respect me. Otherwise you can't train here."

"But my parents told me that if I don't train here then I have to see some shrink to fix the problems I'm having at school."

"Then you have a choice," he told me. "What happens from here on out is up to you, and no one else—not me, not Mom, and not Dad—just you. If you want to avoid seeing a shrink, or whoever else your parents are going to drag you to, then you have to show me respect when we talk. No reverence or obedience, but respect."

"What do those words mean?" I asked.

"You can disagree with me—I'm not some master in a Kung-fu movie from the 1970's. You can have your own mind and your own opinion on things. But how you express those disagreements needs to be done respectfully. Let me be plain with you, Lucas. If you act like an asshole, you're out. Plain and simple, no questions asked. The next drive will be to a psychologist. Simple as that. If you want to avoid that, then I've told you how you need to behave. It's really very simple."

I'd never had anyone take the time to speak to me like that—not yell, not punish, but just give it to me straight, with no emotion involved. I responded to that right away.

"Okay, I get it. And look, I'm sorry, I didn't mean to be an asshole."

"It's okay. But we need to go back to what I was saying. Do you disagree that you're an insecure person?"

"Well, kind of, yeah. I mean, isn't insecurity for girls? I always hear that. *She's sleeping around with half the football team because she's insecure, or has no self esteem.* I've never heard it said about a guy."

"Now you have. And that's only one way insecurity can change the way you behave. For some girls, it's things like you just described, but for boys, it's how you carry yourself."

"And how do I carry myself?" I asked.

"Arrogantly. You act like you're better than everyone, but you don't believe that at all. You think the opposite, actually, so you overcompensate by puffing your chest out and mouthing off to teachers. That's arrogance, and it comes from a lack of confidence."

This dude was blowing my mind, so much so that I actually forgot that we were talking about me. I just got into the things he was saying. "I thought those were the same thing. I mean, not exactly, but I thought that arrogance was just someone with too much confidence."

"No," he told me without missing a step. "That's not true. Confidence is quiet. Confidence just is, and a confident man doesn't have to tell you how great he is at anything, or how much better he is than other people. Only arrogant men do that. Only insecure men."

"You're freaking me out right now."

"Good," he said. It was the first time in all of that time that he really smiled. "If you stick around long enough, I'll do that a lot. But understand that I was just like you. I got into fights. I got into trouble. I was arrogant also. It took someone to take me under their wing and show me that I was wrong about almost everything in my life. Maybe I can help you in that regard."

"Dude, you're like Master Splinter."

"Who?" he asked.

"Master Splinter. Like the Ninja Turtles, you know? He's a rat."

"So, you're calling me a rat?"

"No. . . I mean, I guess, sort of but I. . . dude, it was a compliment. Please don't throw me out."

He laughed hysterically. "I'm not going to throw you out. . . yet." When he'd finished laughing, he just looked at me and waited for an answer.

"Yeah," I finally admit. "I was bullied. For a while. I finally got sick of it and I handled things."

"Did you now? Is that what you call what happened? Handling the situation?"

"Those kids needed to learn a lesson. They'd given me shit since 8th grade and I was fucking sick of it!"

"Excuse me," Matt told me. "Don't curse when you're talking to me. You haven't earned that privilege yet."

"Privilege? Since when is it a privilege to curse?"

"Is it something you want to do?" he asked.

"Yeah."

"Well it's not something I want to listen to. So, if you want to curse, you have to earn it. That makes it a privilege. Outside say whatever the fuck you want, but in here you have to earn your right to be angry."

"But you just. . ."

"I know I did. It's my gym, and I'm older than you."

"That's not fair, man."

"No," he agreed. "From your perspective, I don't suppose it is. But if you're going to be in a martial arts dojo, you have to understand something important. There's a pecking order here. This isn't our soft little society where everyone gets a participation trophy—this is the wild, where every animal knows his place in the pack, and if you forget that place, everyone will remind you. That's what I just did. Don't curse around me. Not until you've earned it."

"Fine, whatever."

"And here's lesson number two—getting into fist fights isn't the way to solve problems. It's just not. If you're going to swing on everyone who picks on you, we're not going to get along."

"But. . ."

"No buts for right now. I need to know that you're not going to get into any fights while you train here. In fact, I want you to do everything you can to avoid situations like that. If you can't agree to those conditions, then you can talk to the psychologist your parents are dying to take you to to deal with your anger issues."

"No, man. I don't want that. Last thing I need is to lie down on some pedophile's couch and have him talk to me about my feelings. I didn't want to hurt them. That's the truth. I just wanted them to stop. That was the only thing that worked."

"I see. Listen, I can't change the past and neither can you. What happened, happened. You can tell me about it or not, but regardless, I'm going to teach you how to be confident—how to trust yourself, and how to be humble. If you stick around, you'll be around enough confident people that maybe you'll learn what it looks like. You can fake it till you make it. I'll help you make it real."

That was ten years ago.

At twenty-five, I've learned most of the lessons that Matt has tried to teach me, but I can still be stubborn and pig headed.

Master Splinter approaches me in the back when I'm getting into my gi and tells me to sit down. "I'm covering your class today. I need you to do something for me."

"What is it?"

"I need you to take on a special case."

"Case? Of what?"

"There's a kid out there—twelve years old—he's being bullied at school and his parents brought him here so that he could learn to defend himself against the kids who are harassing him at school."

"We have a bullying class," I tell him. "Why can't he just take one of those? Kelly can. . ."

"Like I said, this is a special case. He wasn't just bullied,

Lucas, he was beaten—badly. The whole thing was caught on his schools' security camera."

As soon as I hear that, it makes me angry.

I hate bullies.

I'm going to say that again. I-fucking-hate-bullies.

And I don't hate them just because I was bullied myself, I hate how they mess other people up. In some cases, they mess them up for life. People walking around thinking they're less than what they are, all because some prick in the 8th grade made what should have been normal days into living hells. I'll do anything I can to help this kid.

"I want to meet him," I say.

"I thought you might. He's waiting in the lobby with his parents."

CHAPTER FIVE

LUCAS

I can tell the kid has no confidence before I even meet him.

He's not standing with his parents, he's standing *behind* his parents. It's a weird visual because he's a big kid—almost as tall as his father, yet he's cowering behind them like a scared five-year-old. I know right away that I have my work cut out for me.

Matt walks me over to the family, and I read the look of concern and frustration on the mom's face. I extend my hand right away and smile so that I can put them at ease. I can tell that they dragged their kid here out of desperation.

"I'm Lucas, pleased to meet you."

"Steven Bauer," he says, shaking my hand firmly. "This is my wife, Emily."

"Nice to meet you as well. And who's this guy?"

The kid is still hiding. That was my gentle way of trying to get him out from behind his father, but nothing. Dad takes a step to the side and basically pulls the kid out in front where I can look him in the eye—only he won't look me in the eye. He's staring at the floor, and his shoulders are rounded. Everything about this kid screams victim.

"This is our son, Matthew."

I put my hand out again. Matthew takes it, but just barely. It feels like a dead fish in my hand—soft, weak, and more than a little sweaty. He must be nervous. "Welcome to our gym, Matthew. How can I help you guys?"

"I assume Matt told you about our son's. . . about the situation."

"He did. I'm sorry that happened to you all. But you came to the right place."

I try to use a calm voice—calmer than I usually use. I'm not this sweet, and even though I can relate to the idea of being bullied, I was never as much of a victim as Matthew seems to be. He's soft, timid, afraid to angle his head up from the mats. I may have been insecure when I was his age, but not this bad. I feel terrible for the kid.

"Are you going to, like, teach me to fight?" he finally asks.

"I'm not going to teach you anything if you can't look at me, Matthew. Or do you like Matt better?"

"It doesn't matter."

"Matt, then. It's shorter. I like saving time. From now on you're Matt, whether you want to be or not." I get the slightest hint of a smile, and finally he looks up and meets my eyes. "There we go. I was playing a guessing game of what color eyes you had. I win."

"What color did you think they were?"

"No idea," I tell him. "I bet myself that you'd look up before I had to actually guess. So, like I said, I win. But I didn't answer your question, did I?"

"What question?"

"You asked if I was going to teach you how to fight, and the answer is no, I'm not. You're not a fighter."

"I'm sorry," his dad says, interjecting. "But if you're not going to teach our son how to fight then why did we come to a martial arts gym?"

"Because you're scared for him, and I would be too. I'm going to help your son, but I'm not going to teach him how to fight."

"What then?" the mom asks. "Why are we here?"

"Because I am going to teach him how to defend himself. That's not the same thing."

"Wait, I'm confused." I turn to the sound of Matt's voice. "What's the difference?"

"The difference is huge," I tell him. "Look at me, Matt. You see me? I'm a fighter. I came in this gym around your age, well a few years older than you are now, and I learned how to hurt other people—to fight other fighters in a cage for money. I love what I do, but it's not for everyone. You teach people how to fight when you want them to fight. You teach people to defend themselves so that they don't have to fight like me. I learned how to defend myself long before I learned how to fight. That's what I can help you with, but you have to be willing to learn."

"He is," his dad says.

"No disrespect, Steven, but I need to hear it from your son. You can't commit to this for him. He has to be willing to put in the work. Otherwise you're wasting your time and mine. So," I say, looking back at Matt. "How about it? Are we going to do this, or do you want to be a punching bag for the pricks at your school for the next few years?"

"I. . . I want to be able to defend myself, Mr. . ."

"Professor," I say, correcting him. "That's what we call our teachers here. Professor."

"Okay, sorry. I want to be able to defend myself, Professor. Will you please help me?"

"That's what I've been waiting to hear, Matt. And of course I can. Now, first lesson, are you ready?"

"Uh huh."

"Stand up straight."

CHAPTER SIX

MILA

The Following Friday

I get out of my therapy session in just enough time to meet Holly and Sophie at the bar downtown. It's the last thing I feel like doing, but Dr. Chase keeps telling me that I need to get out more. That's not how he says it though. Shrinks have their own language for things that are supposed to be simple. Instead of telling me that it would be good for me to get out of my apartment more often, he tells me that I need to "push past the trauma to get back to a place of self-actualization."

That's shrink code for, *you're still fucked up from your ex-boyfriend nearly killing you, and you might be slightly less fucked up if you grab a drink with friends every once in a while.* I wish he'd just say that to me—I'd respect him more for it. No matter how it comes out, the message is the same, and I'm going to try to be a good patient and follow his advice. That, and the fact that Holly and Sophie have been there for me through this whole ordeal means that the least I can do is sit with them for an hour and sip some wine.

The Uber drops me off at this upscale new bar called Wine-O—I really can't believe they called it that, but at least there's no false advertising going on. There's already a line to get in, like it's a club or something, but I get to feel glamorous and skip the line since Holly texted me that they're both inside at a table already.

Being out is still difficult for me. I start to feel some anxiety rise from my stomach into the rest of my body, and I have to stop walking and remind myself of the self-affirming phrases that Dr. Chase has been working with me on.

You've got this, Mila.

When my heart slows down enough to let me move again, I grind my teeth and just push through the crowd standing in front of the place. Touch has been a trigger of mine since the incident, so I try to avoid any situations where someone touches me. That's why I stopped taking the subway and buses and started dipping into my savings to pay for all the Ubers and taxis. There's no way through the door without touching someone, so I say "excuse me" loud enough to sound rude, and turn my body to the side to avoid anything that might set me off. Once I'm inside I look around and see Holly waving at me.

"We got a table in the perfect spot for you," she tells me after we hug. For some reason the touch thing doesn't apply to Holly and Sophie. They can hug me all they want, or touch me in general, and I don't feel triggered. Probably because I've known them since we were in middle school. She leads me away from the door and continues, "Far back and you can see everyone."

"Perfect. You two are the best. What would I do without you?"

"Shrivel up and die." Sophie realizes what she said as

soon as it's out of her mouth. I feel bad that she feels bad. "Fuck, I'm sorry. I didn't mean. . ."

"It's okay," I tell her. "You can't dance around me forever. I'm a big girl, and I'm getting better. It's been a year."

"That isn't enough time. I'm sorry, I didn't mean to be insensitive."

"It's okay, Soph, you know I love you." I hug her tight to emphasize my point. "And you're not wrong. I might shrivel up and die without you two. You're the only thing keeping me sane these days."

"Us and lots of wine, right?"

Holly isn't wrong. I've been drinking a little too much, and I know it's a coping strategy. I never used to drink at all. What started as a glass of wine with dinner became two glasses, which became a glass whenever I felt like it. It's not doing anything negative in my life—I'm not some drunk who's crashing her car and stumbling around the street slurring words, but I have been using it as a way to numb the pain I still feel. I guess meeting at bar called Wine-O wasn't the best idea.

"Too much," I say. "I'm only having one right now. Red."

"Pinot, we know," Sophie says, finishing my sentence for me. "We have a bottle on the way. Drink your one glass, we'll have the rest."

I smile. It's been a year since I was involved in the scariest thing that's ever happened to me. My boyfriend at the time—now my convict ex, Brett—nearly beat me to death in the apartment we shared downtown. He'd never laid a hand on me before that, and he never showed any of the classic signs of an abusive partner. Brett never tried to isolate me from my friends or family; he never tried to destroy my self-esteem or put me down; and he never even tried to control what I did or who I saw.

Dr. Chase is still baffled by it, but he has an alternative explanation.

Mental illness.

When it came up at trial, introduced by Brett's defense attorney, I thought it was bullshit—a legal trick like you'd see some slimy lawyer pull on an episode of Law & Order —*not guilty by reason of mental defect.* But it turns out Brett had a psychotic disorder that went untreated for years. When his defense team tried to claim mental illness, my lawyer insisted that we have him evaluated by an independent, third party psychologist of our choosing, and the results were clear. On top of that, it came out that Brett did a stint in juvie for assault in high school for beating one of his teachers to a pulp in front of the entire class. His records were expunged because he was a minor at the time, but my lawyer found out about it.

He put me in the hospital for over two months. I still have weird physical issues including some memory problems. I'd tried to defend myself, but realized really quickly that when you don't know how to do that, and a man twice your size wants to hurt you, there isn't a whole lot to do except cover up and hope that you wake up when it's over.

I did wake up, just not the same as I was before.

Our wine comes, and Holly and Sophie do their best to do what they always end up doing when we get together now—ask me how I'm feeling. I'm sick of being treated like a patient of theirs instead of a friend, but I know that they're just concerned for my well being. Sophie has had a glass already—I can tell—and she's the more loose-lipped of my two best friends.

"How was therapy?" she asks. "Are you better yet? When can we meet guys again?"

"Jesus, Sophie!" Holly yells.

"No, it's okay." I'm actually happy to hear a normal question for once. "Ummm... I'm not dating anyone yet, Sophie. Brett was only convicted five months ago. I'm having trouble even leaving my house, and my anxiety is through the roof. I'm not sure any guy would find my being an anxious hermit attractive."

I'm pretending like it's a real answer I'm giving her—I'm playing along with what's socially expected of me—to be normal. But the real answer to her question is something I'm not ready to say out loud. Something I'm not fully ready to admit to myself.

No, Sophie, I won't be meeting any new guys because Brett fucked me up so bad that I'm scared of almost every man I meet—literally. The barista at Starbucks, the men who pass me on the street. Shit, even my own therapist took some getting used to. I think every man is going to hurt me now, so I either need to avoid them altogether, or go live on some all female island like Wonder Woman. Other than that, I'm totally fucked when it comes to men!

I take a sip of my Pinot and think about what she just asked me. The truth is I do miss being with someone, even though it's not on my radar at the moment. But the feeling of having someone in my bed—having that sense of security and being in love, I miss that. I take another sip.

"Moving on. . ." Holly says, shooting Sophie a look of irritation. "How are things, otherwise? Not dating, but just you. How are you?"

I take a deep breath because it's a hard question, but I'm going to do my best to answer it. "I'm doing. . . better. If I'm being honest, I'm still a little south of good, but I'm north of terrible. Wherever that is, that's where I am."

"That's great, Mila. I wish I could program my GPS to that location all the time. Being super happy all the time is overrated—it's a fantasy we tell ourselves. I'm happy to just be okay."

"That's the thing, though, Holl, I still have so many of the after effects of the attack that I wish would just fucking go away. The worry, the stress, the anxiety, even the paranoia. I want it to just stop so I can feel like myself again. I miss me."

"I miss the old you, too. I miss going out, spending more time together. But we both get it. All of that is secondary to you getting better. It's a process, Mila—and you're doing great."

"She's right," Sophie says. "We love you, and you're doing really well."

"I love you guys, too. And thank you for being there through all of it."

"I was about ready to have my mail forwarded to that hospital room," Holly says. "I spent more time there than I did at my place."

"You guys really are the best."

"Question," Holly says suddenly. "Do you trust me?"

"Of course I do, why?"

"Oh, Jesus," Sophie says. "Here it comes. She was talking about this before you got here."

"What is it?" I ask.

"You know how you said you need your confidence back? How you're scared and wish that you weren't?"

"Yeah."

"Well—I know you're doing great in therapy and all, but I have another idea to help you."

I see the look on her face and I know she's up to no good.

I guess I'll just have to wait and see.

CHAPTER SEVEN

LUCAS

I can't sleep.

I should be sleeping. But what happened in my last fight is still fucking with my head. Every night, when the lights go out, it's all I think about. Not only do I relive the experience of being woken up, but I've seen the footage of the fight more times than I can count. I'm obsessed with my own defeat. I haven't stepped back in that cage in a year, and I'm itching for a fight.

A lot of people use the expression 'it keeps me up at night', but for me it's literal. I run through the fight in my head—what I could have done differently, what I did wrong, what I would do if I had that opportunity again. All of those thoughts equal no sleep or bad sleep, which isn't the best thing for training, but I can't help it.

I fucking hate to lose.

Not only is my pride and ego still hurt, but I feel like I let my team down—Matt, and all the guys who put countless hours into making me into a champion. I let them all down by not keeping my hands where they should have been. Amateur hour stuff. Fuck, I owe them more than that. I owe them my destiny—a championship belt to hang on the gym walls. That's what I deserve. That's what this gym deserves.

It's late, but I call up Matt.

"Hello?"

"Hey man, it's me. Sorry to bother you so late."

"What fuckin' time is it?"

"Umm... three fifteen."

"Are you dying?" he asks. "You'd better be for waking me up at this time."

"I want another fight."

"Lucas. . ."

"No, man. I want another fight. I need to get back into the win column."

"You're still under medical suspension, right?"

"Nah, those passed a while back. I'm good. It was only six months."

There are protocols when a fighter is knocked out— usually mandatory amounts of time where you're medically suspended and can't get licensed again until that time is up. I set a reminder on my phone because I knew Matt would ask about it. He wanted me to take even more time off because of the knockout, but I can't wait any longer.

"I need this, Matt. I need it so bad I can taste it. And I need you to help me find an opponent."

"Are you sure you're ready for that already? That was a bad knockout."

"Yeah it was. I fucked up, and I'm sorry. I need a chance to make it right. I need to make another run at that title."

Matt hears the urgency in my voice. He's heard that

tone before and he knows that there's no talking me out of it. "Alright. I'll work on it, okay? But I need you to do something for me in exchange."

"Name it."

"I need you to do a private tomorrow."

"Oh, fuck, not another one?" I ask. "I worked with that kid again today, now another? Enough of this shit."

"Yeah, asshole. Now another. Kaitlyn was supposed to do it but she had something come up. I need you to cover for me. It's an important one—a favor for a friend of my wife."

"Okay. Who is it?"

"A woman. Her friend's bringing her in for some self-defense Jiu Jitsu. I told her I'd give her an intro class for free, and if she likes it I'll let her take a few more privates. From what I heard she's kind of delicate."

"Delicate?" I repeat "Are you sure I'm the right guy for someone like that? I'm not exactly Mr. Sensitivity."

He laughs on the other end of the phone. "Like you had to tell me that. You are many things, kid, but sensitive is not a word I'd use to describe you. But you are a great teacher, the kids and their parents love you in the anti-bullying classes. Plus, there's no one else, so I need you to step up for me."

"Fine." I tell him. "I'll step up, but I'd really appreciate if you could do the same and make some calls tomorrow about a match?"

"You got it. I'll do it right after I make up for all the sleep you just deprived me of."

"You're an animal, Matt, you'll be up at five, don't lie."

"You're not wrong. And goodnight. Thanks for taking the private tomorrow. Be gentle with this one tomorrow, alright?"

"Of course," I joke. "Gentle is my middle name. Oh, speaking of names, what's hers?"

"Mila. Now go to bed."

Mila. I like that. I wonder if she's as beautiful as her name.

CHAPTER EIGHT

MILA

Saturday Morning

I don't know why Holly dragged me to this place.

I mean, I do know why. She means well, and I know that she wants me to get over what happened with Brett, but I'm not sure this whole thing is really my speed.

My body's healed up—mostly—and now the battle is for control of my mind. It's my mind that's still covered in bandages and lying in traction. I never thought that Brett would be capable of something like that—and I sure as hell never believed that I'd be the type of woman stuck in a situation like that. But he was, and so was I. And now here I am, in the passenger seat of Holly's car, parking in front of a martial arts gym, of all places. The awning reads:

New York Fight Club: Mixed Martial Arts

"I don't get it, why do I have to do this?" I sound whiny. I hate the tone in my voice because I sound like a kid being dragged shopping by her mom.

"I told you. I've been taking classes here for over a year. They have an amazing self-defense program for women and kids. I've taken like three different types of classes and I'm practically a badass."

"I'm scared of you."

"You should be." She jokes. "But seriously, they have great instructors, and this isn't that old school self defense where they tell you to yell and stab the guy with your keys—this Jiu Jitsu stuff really works. It really helps with your self confidence, and I know that's just what you need that right now."

"I'm not a karate fighter, Holly. I've seen those movies and trust me, none of that flying stuff would have helped me when Brett was on top of me, slamming his fists down."

It upsets me to even say that. This is maybe the second or third time I've ever said anything directly about what happened, outside of my police report, testimony in court, and to Dr. Chase. That testimony—plus the injuries I was still nursing at the time—was enough to send him away for a few years. Not nearly enough, in my opinion. But Brett has a lot of money and a great attorney. My lawyer wasn't able to meet the burden of proof necessary for a charge of attempted murder, which is what he should have been charged with. So instead we got him convicted of the lesser crime of aggravated assault. They played the mental health thing up as much as they could.

Holly takes my hand gently. "Sweetie, you're thinking of Bruce Lee movies right now. Or maybe Jean Claude Van Damme—he's the guy with the accent who does the splits, right?"

"I have no idea, Holly, you know I'm bad with movies."

"I do know. I don't know what I was thinking. It doesn't matter—if you're thinking of some guy in robes doing spinning back kicks and flying through the air then you're thinking of the wrong thing. First, this isn't a karate school, it's a Mixed Martial Arts academy."

"Wait, what's the difference?"

"There are a lot. Karate is... well, it's karate. It's a traditional Japanese martial art that has an academy on every corner and strip mall in the United States."

"So, what's this place, then?"

"You have so much to learn, Mila. But that's kind of why we're here," Holly says with a slight chuckle.

"I really don't know about this. What am I going to be doing, exactly? Maybe if you walk me through it so I don't feel like I'm walking into something weird."

"I have a better idea," she tells me. "Why don't we go in and meet a guy named Matt. He's the owner and also the head trainer of the real fighters. I went to high school with his wife. We're not close or anything—basically only slightly more than Facebook friends at this point, but he treats me like I'm family and gives me a great discount. He's good with finding people the right trainer to work with. I called him the other day to see if he was able to find you someone."

"And did he?" I'm starting to warm to the idea a little. I trust Holly and I know she has my best interest at heart. If she says this place is legit then I'm going to trust her.

"He said there's a retired female fighter who does private lessons and training stuff now. Should be good. Thing is, we have to actually go inside to find out."

"Shut up," I joke. "I'm going to go in. I just feel stupid. How is this going to help me?"

"I guess we'll just have to find out. Can we get out of the car now? I scheduled you an introductory lesson that starts in ten minutes and you need to get changed."

"Fine, I'm trusting you," I tell her. "But if I hate it, I don't want you to drag me back a second time. Deal?"

"Deal. Now get your lazy ass out of the car."

"Yes, ma'am."

My heart is racing again, just like it does now whenever I'm forced to be around people. Travel is one thing, but when I'm in a confined space with a group of people my anxiety comes back full force. I never thought that I'd be that person—the agoraphobic who lived their life terrified that something bad was going to happen. What sucks is that I was never like that—I'm an extrovert by nature—I used to love parties, talking to people, going out dancing—whatever it was. It wasn't until my attack that I developed all these fears and insecurities. I hope this will help me get over all of that.

As soon as we step inside I hear a man's voice yell out. It startles me a little, but it's a friendly voice. "Holly! How are you?" She runs over and hugs the man who I assume is. . .

"Matt! I'm great!"

After they separate, they both turn towards me. Matt's a big guy, and his ears looks like he's fought a few times in his life. He's got those things—I forget what they're called—but it's like when it looks like there's a big tumor on the inside of your ears. I had a boyfriend in college who wrestled and he had them. I'll have to ask Holly what they're called later on. Speaking of my best friend, she waves me over and Matt goes to shake my hand.

"And this must be the one and only Mila?"

"That's me." I shake his hand, and he really *shakes* my hand. It's the first thing I notice—a lot of guys will lighten their grip when they shake a woman's hand, but not this one. He gives me a good squeeze.

"Welcome to my gym. Holly's told me about your. . .situation. I'm happy to help you in any way that I can.

"Thank you. I'm glad to be here, I really appreciate you taking the time to have your people work with me."

"It's my honor. And just so you know, just for privacy reasons, I didn't share your information with your instructor just yet, in case you didn't want your business spread around. He'll be here in a minute. He's on his way, just running a little late."

He? Did Matt just call my instructor a he?

"I'm sorry," I say, feeling the anxiety rise again. "Holly told me that I'd have a woman instructor. Is she not here?"

"Oh, I'm sorry, I forgot to text Holly. That instructor had to cancel last minute—she got sick last night with some bad food poisoning. Instead I'm giving you over to Lucas. He's a pro fighter—maybe you've heard of him? Lucas 'The Ghost' Esparza?"

"Can't say that I have, no, I'm sorry. I don't really know fighters."

"That's okay. If you feel like it you can look him up while we wait if you want. He should be here any minute."

As soon as I hear there's going to be a man putting his hands all over me I feel uncomfortable all over again, but I feel like there's no turning back now. I hope this isn't a disaster.

While I wait for the very late Lucas Esparza, I take out my phone and go on YouTube. I type in *'Lucas The Ghost Esparza fight'* into the search and watch the first video. It's titled 'Viscous KO' – I turn the volume down and click on the video. It's only twenty seconds long, but in almost no time I see a guy who I think is my instructor get kicked in the head and fall to the floor. He lies there while the other guy celebrates. It's hard to watch, and I flinch when I see the blow.

"Holy crap!" I yell without even thinking.

"What is it?" Holly asks.

"Nothing. Just saw something weird online." I close my phone and try to cover what I just saw.

"Isn't everything you see online weird in one way or the other?"

"I guess."

We stand and talk to Matt for about five minutes before Holly convinces me to sit on the floor with her and stretch a little bit, so that's exactly what I do. We stretch for another five minutes before I see a guy walk in the front door with a bag slung over his shoulder. I don't think my eyes are going to leave him for a while.

The first thing I notice is his size—he's so big—tall, really muscular, and hot as all fuck. His body is one thing, but it's his face that really catches my attention. His cheekbones are high, and they frame his entire face. His looks are a mix of gentle and rugged—like if a Versace model and a really tough athlete had a baby. The contrast intrigues me. He's like a beautiful photo that's just slightly out of focus—and I stare at him as he approaches us. When I stand up to greet him I have to angle my neck to look up.

"Hey," he says. His tone is curt, and more than a little bit cocky.

"Hey, Lucas," Holly says. "This is my friend Mila. She's all yours today."

"Right. Great."

He really couldn't sound more disinterested. Does he not want to do this?

"Hi," I say, putting my hand out to shake. "I'm Mila."

I'm not a hand-shaker, but I don't know what else to do. When he doesn't shake back and bows at me instead I get the message. I try to bow, but end up looking down at the ground. That's when I feel his two fingers underneath my chin, lifting it up to meet his piercing green eyes.

"Here," he says, pointing to his own eyes. "Always here. Never look down when you bow." His eyes are captivating—and I stare a little too long. "And nice to meet you, Mila."

"Oh, okay, sorry."

"Be gentle with her." Holly says. "I was telling her before you came in that she's in good hands with you."

"Stop lying to your friend." He says. When he speaks I can't tell if he's being dry and sarcastic, or just really rude and dismissive. "Now leave us alone."

Holly gives me a hug and walks away, and when she does I feel naked, like a kid who's been abandoned by his mom in a crowd. I'm in the middle of a strange gym, surrounded by sweaty men making weird grunting sounds while they hit things, and now this big guy is looking at me like I'm supposed to know what to do. *Should I, like, bow again or something? How does it work?*

"So, you're here to learn self defense?" he asks.

"I think so. I mean, that's what Holly thinks I should do."

"Is Holly your mom? Do you always let her make your decisions for you?"

Did he really just say that? Is he being a dick to me? "Uh. . . no, definitely not my mom, and what I mean is that she suggested that I come here."

"And you disagree? You don't want to be here?"

What the hell is this guy's problem? "I. . . I 'm honestly not sure."

"Okay, well then why don't you leave? I have other things to do that aren't a complete waste of my time."

"Excuse me?"

"You heard me. I train people who want to learn. If you're not into it then go do something else. I'm a busy man, I fight for a living."

I don't remember the last time someone spoke to me the way he's speaking to me. He's brash, arrogant, and he has a really bad attitude for a teacher. But at the same time, I can't stop looking at him. It's weird.

"Look, I'm into it," I tell him. "I just don't really know what *it* is exactly. Since you're the instructor and all, and since I've never done this before, how about you explain *it* to me."

"Well, *it* is a type of martial art called Brazilian Jiu Jitsu. It's a grappling art."

"Grappling?"

"No punching or kicking. It's more about manipulating other people's bodies and using their strength against them."

Speaking of bodies. . . even though this guy is being really obnoxious, he has the body of a Greek god underneath that gi. The lapels are slightly open, and he's not wearing a shirt underneath. Every time he shifts his weight to one foot the flaps open, and his pecks are staring at me—well defined, and sitting over the most perfect six pack—shit, it might be an eight pack—that I've ever seen on a man. Holy shit.

"Oh, okay. So, show me something that'll save my life."

"Gladly. Let's start with me mounting you."

"Excuse me?" I ask, my eyes wide open and my body secretly intrigued by what he just said. "You want to mount me?"

"Not until I get to know you better," he jokes. I don't

react at all. "But for real, that's the name of a position. It's called 'full mount'."

"Oh. Right. Sure."

"Lie down."

Yes, sir. Gladly.

I do what he says, and I take in just how he says it. I know he's showing me a technique, but in the back of my mind I imagine him really telling me to lie down—and I don't hate it. I fall to my back, and he literally mounts me, throwing one leg over me until his crotch is pressing down on my stomach and his hips are above mine. He has to weigh over two hundred pounds, but he moves like a gazelle and is barely putting any weight on me. I'm helpless underneath him nonetheless, and I just lie still and wait as he explains the position to me.

"This is the full mount. It's one of the worst positions you can find yourself in if someone attacks you, do you know why?"

"Because I'm helpless." I force the memory of Brett on top of me from my mind.

"Right. I can hit you from here." I try to hide my involuntary flinch as he makes a fist and extends it down towards my face, his knuckles just barely touching my chin. "But you can't hit me. Try to reach your hand up." I do what he says, and with my arm fully extended I'm still a few inches from his face. "Plus, I have control of your body."

"Okay, so how do I get out of it?"

"Ah, good, now you're asking the right question. Let me show you."

And he does.

He shows me how to escape—a move called the 'trap and roll', and after that he shows me some more quick self defense moves—things to do if a larger person like him grabbed me from behind, or put their hands around my throat. I'm really interested in everything he's showing me, and now I get why Holly thought this would be a good idea. These are things that every woman should know, whether she's experienced what I went through or not. Hopefully not. Hopefully never—but it's good to know these moves, just in case.

We go for about twenty minutes more before he decides to test me. "Alright, you did good. But the question is, how well do you think you remember what I just showed you?"

"Everything? I'm not sure. . ."

"Imagine you walked out of here today and someone grabbed you. Someone big, like me." *So, someone just like my ex? Got it.* "What would you do?"

"Hopefully I'd do what you just showed me."

"Let's see."

When Lucas was teaching me those moves, he was humble. Beyond. He was patient, showed me my mistakes, broke everything down step by step, and repeated himself as many times as I needed him to. But right now—and like before—he's back to being his cocky self. I'm not sure which version I like. Part of me hates arrogant men, but there's something about Lucas's type of cockiness that has me looking at him like I haven't looked at man in a long time. He seems like the opposite of me—like nothing could rattle him.

"Wait," I say, a little nervous. "How are we going to do that?"

"I'm going to pretend to be the fake robber or rapist. I'm going to grab you, and you're going to try and do any one or more of the moves we just drilled to try to get out of it. Understand?"

I nod because I don't know what else to do, but when he

says it like that, I get really uncomfortable for some reason. I feel strangely comfortable with Lucas, and I had no issue with him touching me or literally being on top of me moments ago, but I start to feel my old friend anxiety as soon as he frames it like an attack. I know it's fake, I know it's an exercise, but part of me feels like I'm not. . .

"Ready? Here we go."

Before I have time to protest or explain myself, he positions himself behind me. I instinctively stay still, waiting for him to put his hands on me as my anxiety rises. I should stop this whole thing—walk away and explain the situation so that he understands why this isn't a good idea, but something in me just freezes. That's when I feel his big arms come over my shoulders and drape across my chest like he's going to choke me. And that's exactly when I freak the fuck out.

I scream.

Not a polite little yell. Not a pull away to let him know I'm not okay yell. I scream like he's really an attacker and I'm really being attacked. The anxiety becomes a fight-or-flight response without me even realizing it, and I turn into him and push with all the strength I have in my body. Even with the adrenaline coursing through me, I can barely move Lucas an inch—he's too big and too solid, but I try anyway because I'm insane right now.

Everyone looks over, and once Lucas puts his hands up like he's surrendering, my brain finally calms down. And once I'm calm, the embarrassment starts to settle in. I look around the room and everyone is watching me, and I start to get really angry at myself. Only instead of just letting myself feel that, I externalize it.

"What the hell do you think you're doing?" I scream.

Lucas opens his eyes and looks at me. "Huh? What am I doing?"

"Yes!"

"I was trying to test how much you learned so that you could leave here and use a self-defense technique if you needed to."

"Well that's a shitty way to do that—just grabbing someone like that."

"Mila." I'm so crazy that I barely hear my name being called—I just turn to the feeling of a soft hand on my shoulder. "It's just me." Holly is standing behind me looking horrified. She takes her hand back right away, probably because she's worried I'll flip out again. I feel so embarrassed.

"Look, lady. . ."

"It's Mila!" I yell back at Lucas. "What kind of teacher doesn't remember his student's name? But I guess you miss things a lot."

He looks at me a little more sharply—almost curiously. "What the hell does that even mean?"

"Well you missed that blow that knocked you out in your last fight. I just watched it on YouTube."

"Mila!"

I don't need Holly's reprimand to know that I went way too far. This man didn't do anything wrong, and I just gave him a verbal strike right to the balls. He just looks at me. He doesn't yell back. Doesn't scream. Doesn't tell me to go screw myself and to never come back to his gym. He just looks at me in total silence. That's when I turn around and storm out. No more words. No more embarrassment. I turn my body around and walk out and wait by Holly's car. She follows me out a second later.

"Mila, what the hell happened in there? You looked like you were having a good time."

"I'm so sorry," I tell her. "When he grabbed me like that it just reminded me. . ." I start crying. I can't help it. That's when I fall into Holly's arms. She squeezes without needing any more of an explanation from me. It's a best friend hug. It's all I need right now.

CHAPTER NINE

LUCAS

What an absolute bitch! A hot bitch, but still, that doesn't make up for it.

I can't believe that she brought up my last fight a few minutes after I met her! I didn't say anything back because she's obviously screwed up and I'm not about to bully some mentally ill chick. But, still, the balls on her to freak out on me like that. As soon as she stormed out, I grabbed Matt and pulled him into the back to have a talk about it.

"What the absolute fuck, dude? You setting up privates at the mental institution now?"

"I'm sorry, I had no idea. . ."

"Wait," I said, interrupting him. "Didn't you say something about her last night? Like she was a metal case or something?"

"Not quite what I said, but you're not totally off. What I told you was that she was fragile, delicate."

"And is 'fragile' Master Splinter code for 'crazy bitch'? 'Cause that's what she was out there. Did you see everyone staring? Did you hear what she said?"

"Yes and yes. Everyone did. And I can't get into it, so please don't ask, but she's been through a lot, and she's clearly not totally over it just yet. Try to be patient and understand that."

"So, am I done with privates now? Can I just focus on fighting? If that's not a prime example of why I should be training on the mats and not teaching on them I don't know what is."

"First off, I'm sorry she did that. If I'd known she was going to have that reaction I wouldn't have given her to you. Holly told me that Mila was doing better, so that's on me. But, as to your other question, no, you're not done. Teaching is part of this gym—you'll always do it as long as I'm your trainer."

"Great," I said sarcastically.

"But, I will definitely pull back your schedule the closer we get to a fight. Best I can offer."

"Then I guess it'll have to do."

That was earlier in the day. Now it's midnight and I can't sleep—again. I'm not angry at what happened, more shocked than anything. Lucky for her, I don't offend easily. Having a thick skin is a big part of being a fighter. How mad could I be? She was telling the truth, but she still shocked my ass.

But it's not my ass I'm thinking of right now. It's her ass.

Mila was annoying, but there was something about her that I can't stop thinking of. I haven't had a girlfriend in over a year—and and I'm using that word pretty loosely. It's hard to be a professional fighter and have time for a relationship. Unless you're dating another fighter, most women just don't know how much time you have to spend at the gym to get to the highest levels of this game. It's hard to find someone who's understanding enough to deal with you never being around.

That's why I've had a lot of women, but not a lot of legit girlfriends. Speaking of those women—when I was on my winning streak I had them lined up. It was like I was in Motley Crue back in the day. The girls would wait outside the fights to introduce themselves, or follow our team to the after party at whatever bar I was drinking at after a win—and I'm pretty sure I hit just about every single one at some point. I liked to party.

Lying here in bed I'm not thinking of my partying days, and I'm sure as fuck not thinking about a relationship right now—I'm focused on the giant hard on I have thinking of her sweet ass pushing into my crotch as I walked her through some self-defense drills. I think about her mouth as she her straddled over me, and how hard it was to concentrate on technique when all I wanted to do was strip her clothes off, grab her by the hips and have her. . .

Snap out of it, Lucas!

I didn't even realize it at first, but there are little beads of sweat gathered on my forehead. That, and my boxer briefs feel about two sizes too small for me with my cock popping against them. How did that woman have such an effect on me? I literally can't stop thinking about her. She was annoying. She was rude. She was. . . fucking hot.

I don't know what she got out of the whole thing, and why she stormed off like that, but I kind of hope that she comes back another time. Who am I kidding? Who's ever stormed out of the gym then come back again? No one.

Oh well, at least I'll always have the memory of today, and a little something to dream about once I finally get to sleep.

CHAPTER TEN

MILA

The Next Day

I feel awful.

I was a real bitch to that instructor Lucas. He was just trying to do his job—he didn't know about. . . the incident. I wish he did know, because, maybe if he did, he wouldn't have been so aggressive about me trying things, and I wouldn't have flipped out or stormed off. But I liked him, despite the fact that he was a prick. I don't know what it was —maybe his self-assurance, or his knowledge, but he had an energy that really drew me in, even though the other part of my brain was an anxious mess.

I want to go back and take more lessons.

And it's not just to learn self defense.

I hate to admit this to myself—but I found Lucas really attractive. I hated his cockiness, but it also intrigued me. The confidence that came off of him was like no one I've ever seen before. I guess fighters have that, especially ones as big and as good as Lucas must be. He showed me some amazing moves like it was nothing, and then he had the confidence to let me do them on him.

I liked having my hands on him. I like him having his hands on me even more. . .until I freaked out. God! I need to get over this anxiety shit!

But it wasn't just the martial arts that made me feel good yesterday. My body hasn't felt anything like I experienced yesterday with a guy in a very long time. I wasn't even sure if I was capable of that feeling any more since everything happened with Brett, but it was unmistakable. Lucas was kind of a jerk, but part of me liked that. Plus, he's tall, muscular, and can beat the shit out of almost anyone.

When he got on top of me like that, part of me forgot we were in a gym, and I just wanted to open up his gi so that I could feel the pecs that were peaking out from underneath the open lapels of his gi. I don't know what's come over me— I went from fantasy to crazy freak out in no time at all. And on top of that, I was really rude to him. I should never have said what I said about him losing his last fight. That was a really low blow, and I feel like an asshole for going there.

It's not the same thing at all, but I know what it's like to get beaten unconscious and to wake up not knowing what the hell happened. I know what that did to my body and mind, and I understand he signed up for that possibility, but it was still something that I shouldn't have said to him.

I want to make it right. He was trying to help me and I lashed out.

As soon as I get my ass out of bed and shower, I'm heading back there to apologize.

I hope he accepts.

Even if he doesn't, I can't wait to look at him again.

CHAPTER ELEVEN

LUCAS

I have my work cut out for me with this kid.

Our first actual lesson has nothing to do with fighting—and it had everything to do with body language. "You need to stand up straight," I tell him. "You slouch. You also have bad eye contact. I want you to practice looking people in the eye when they're talking to you. That's your homework."

"I get homework?"

"You do. That's it. Shoulders back, better eye contact. You'd be surprised what a difference that will make."

"What do those things matter?"

"You ever watch those Nature Channel documentaries —like the ones in Africa that follow a pride of lions or something?"

"Yeah, I have."

"Let me ask you a question. When those lions hunt, do you ever see them going after other lions?"

"No," he says, laughing a little. "Of course not."

"And when they hunt gazelles, or whatever, do they ever go after the biggest, strongest male in the group?"

"No."

"Right. Who do they go after?"

"The weak ones. Usually the babies or the sick ones."

"Exactly," I say. "And why do you think that is?"

"Because it's easier. Less work and they get to eat."

"Now do you get my point about your posture and eye contact?"

"So, you're saying I'm like a sick baby gazelle? Easy prey."

"Easy prey. Don't make yourself easy. Make yourself look like a challenge—a fight that isn't worth the effort. That alone will solve 95% of your issues. The other five is what we'll work on here. But I don't ever want to see you looking down at your shoes when you're talking again, you hear me?"

"Yes, Professor."

"Good.

He's like a soft ball of putty, and I need him to toughen up. I don't know too many ways that are better than a run. He looks at me like I'm crazy when I tell him.

"I don't really run," he tells me.

"Now you do. Let's go."

A mile later, he's about ready to collapse. He's an overweight kid. Right or wrong, that's another box to check for bullies. Losing weight will be part of our journey together. After we finish our run a little bit from the gym, he falls over and looks like he's about to puke.

"You okay?"

"Yes, Professor. I've never really run before."

I laugh. He looks like he's about to die. "Yeah, I can tell. You'll be okay. I had no stamina when I started training, either."

"You're a fighter, right? Like a real one?"

"I'd like to think so, yeah. Like a real one. But I used to be just like you. I used to get fucked with at school all the time. Fucked me up." I probably shouldn't be saying 'fuck' so much around a kid—I should be a good influence and all that, but I can't help myself. I have a terrible mouth.

"You? Really? I'd never think. . ."

"That someone could bully me? Think again, kid. I was a late bloomer—short through most of school, scrawny, and I looked down a lot, just like you. I was the sick baby gazelle, and there were a lot of lions. There are always a lot of lions."

"I didn't realize. It sounds messed up, but if you turned out this way then maybe there's some hope for me."

I feel bad for the kid. I can tell he's nice and really smart. He just happens to be forced to share space with pricks who make him less than he could be. It's not okay, and I'm gonna do everything I can to help lift him up. "There's always hope. Never forget that. And I was thinking, even though you're not going to fight-fight, like me, it might be cool if you had a fighter nickname. Everyone at the gym has one, and since you're taking private lessons with me, you shouldn't be any different."

"What do you mean?" he questions.

"Like a nickname. In between your first and last. You ever watch MMA or boxing?"

"No. I don't like fighting."

"Alright," I say, realizing that I asked a stupid question. I can't even imagine this kid sitting in front of a TV watching two guys fight in a cage. "Well have you ever heard of Mike Tyson?"

"Yeah, of course, that dude from 'The Hangover', right?"

Oh. Sweet. Jesus. "My man, did you just refer to

arguably the greatest heavyweight boxing champion of all time as 'that dude from The Hangover?'"

"That's where I know him from. I remember he punched Zach Galifianakis, right? That makes sense now!"

"Holy shit, kid, are you kidding?"

"Ummm... sir... I mean Professor. . . I don't think you're supposed to curse at me."

"Well I'm sorry, kid but it's a sin to think that Iron Mike Tyson is just 'that guy who punched Zach Galifianakis' in some movie. I mean, yeah, he is that guy, but the whole reason he was even put in the movie was because he's one of the most devastating hitters of all time."

"Oh, wow. Didn't realize."

I roll my eyes at the kid and exhale dramatically. "Boy, you've got a lot to learn about combat sports. But we can get into that another day. Your parents didn't send you to me for a history lesson. But you still need a cool name. My point with the whole Tyson thing is that his nickname was "Iron." Evander "Real Deal" Holyfield, "The Notorious" Conor McGregor."

"Oh, yeah, I know him. The Irish guy."

"Right. The Irish guy."

"What's your nickname?" he asks.

"The Ghost. I'm Lucas 'The Ghost' Esparza."

"Did you choose it?"

"You never choose your own nickname, kid. It has to be given to you. Matt, the gym owner, gave me mine. He's also my head trainer."

"Why 'ghost'?"

"Because I've always had really good footwork. When guys go to hit me, I'm usually not there. I'm invisible in there, like a ghost."

"Oh, I see, that's really cool. But why do I need one?"

"Are you arguing with your professor?"

"No," he says, looking down. He can't tell that I'm kidding around with him so I back off the stern routine. I joke around a lot and Matt's a little fragile. Don't want to scare him—that's not the point of all this.

"I'm joking, Matt, relax. Remember what I told you about breathing?"

"You mean to do it?" he smiles. It's nice to see a sense of humor underneath all that fear. He's probably a great kid who's learned how to hide himself after he started getting bullied. That's what that shit does to you. It makes you retreat into yourself so you don't get hurt.

"Right," I say, smiling back. "Always remember to breathe. Especially when you're under stress. That's when your body will try to not breathe, and that's when it needs oxygen the most. Always breathe."

"Okay, Professor. I'll try."

"Now, since you and my head trainer have the same name, we need to give you a nickname so that I can keep you two straight."

"But I don't look anything like. . ."

"Remember that relaxing thing I just mentioned? It's a joke."

"Right." He smiles again. "Sorry. Been a while since I was relaxed."

"I get it, and I have an idea. Since you have the same name as my trainer, and that's super confusing, I'm going to call you Matt "The Second" Bauer, from now on."

"But I don't think I like. . ."

"Don't argue with your professor. Now let's go inside and practice."

Matt "The Second" is out of shape, and he might be

the most uncoordinated dude I've ever met, but he's absorbing everything I'm saying like a sponge. He listens, and he's got a good attitude, much better than when he first walked through the doors. I don't know if I'll be able to keep working with him when—and if—I go into fight camp, but we'll have to wait and see. If not, I can pass him off to one of the other guys or girls at the gym.

When we're doing training, I do what I always do with my students before passing him off to his dad, who's waiting outside the gym in his car.

"What did we learn today?"

"That I can't run for shit."

"No!" I yell. I want to smack him upside the head but I'll get in trouble if his dad sees that. So, instead I put my hand on his shoulder and lean over so we're eye to eye. "You didn't learn that because I'm guessing you already knew that you couldn't run for shit. If you could, you'd be on your school's track team or something. That's not what you learned. Think again."

He does. He really does. I see him trying to search his brain for the answer I think he wants, but he comes up with nothing.

"Well, no offense professor, but we didn't do anything except run a lot. I didn't learn any fighting stuff, so I'm not sure what to say to your question."

"First off, remember what I told you—I'm not here to teach you how to fight. What am I going to teach you?"

"Self confidence."

"Right. And confidence comes from pushing past your limits, pushing way farther than you think you're capable of, and coming out on the other side a better kid—a better man. So, before you go get in your dad's car, I'm going to ask you one more time, and this time I want the right answer, whatever you think that might be."

"Okay."

"What did you learn today?"

He stops and thinks again, only this time he looks me in the eye and tells me what I want to hear. "I learned that I can run farther than I thought I could, and that I'm okay. I could do it again if I had to."

"That a boy!" I say, patting him on the shoulder. "Now you can go. And, by the way, we will be doing it again, and next time even farther. Plus, we'll learn some 'fight stuff', like you call it."

"Thanks, Professor, see you next week."

"You got it Matt "The Second," see you then. Keep making eye contact, and keep your damn back straight!"

The kid takes off and Matt calls me into his office. I'm hoping he has some fight news. I'm too impatient to wait. "Tell me what I want to hear, brother."

"I made some calls."

"And? Do I get a rematch?"

Matt looks at me like I just lost my mind. His left eyebrow shoots up and he does what he always does when I say outrageous shit—he takes his glasses off and rubs his eyes. "A rematch is going to be a hard sell, Lucas."

"Why? 'Cause of the knockout?"

"The knockout for one, but even more than that. Wes isn't with New York Cage Fighting anymore. He got the call up."

The call up. That's gym code for him being offered a UFC contract by Sean. It means he's out of the small shows and onto the biggest show of them all. It means he's living one of my greatest dreams. But I can't hate on the guy, he earned his shot. Now, it's time to work my way back up to earning mine.

"Fuck," I say, a little disappointed. "So, what then?"

"I talked to John—he said that if you're healthy and cleared to fight, he has something for you. But you're not going to like who it's against."

"No," I say. "Don't fucking say it."

"Uh-huh."

I don't even need to wait for him to speak his name—Jason "The GOAT" Diaz. He handed me my only loss a few years back when we were both on the amateur circuit, then he got popped for steroids in his first few pro fights. He didn't even feel human when I fought him—the guy was one giant muscle who definitely outweighed me on fight night. There have been rumors about that guy for years. He's as dirty as they come—an unfortunate reality of our sport—and he's the last guy I want to have to deal with again.

"He's being tested rigorously," Matt says.

I let out a dismissive laugh. I don't mean to be a dick, but this low-level testing doesn't mean shit. "How can you look at me with a straight face and say that, Matt? Rigorous? What does that even mean in these shows? They looked at him and figured he probably isn't doing anything, then made him pee in a cup one time after telling him when they were gonna test him? Rigorous like that?"

"I know, it's not the best. . ."

"Not the best? You're damn right. I don't want to fight that roid-head again."

"He didn't pop for your fight. We don't know if he. . ."

"Stop, man. Don't insult either of our intelligences. You think he started doping six months after he beat me? He looked like the Incredible Hulk then, and he still does. It's not a fair fight."

Performance enhancing drugs is a trigger for me. There are so many of them floating around this sport that it makes the Lance Armstrong scandal look tame by comparison. In the old days, literally everyone was doing it. If you go back and look at footage of those guys, they all look like they're training for Mr. Olympia. None of it was natural. Sure, they worked hard and a lot of the guys came from combat sports backgrounds, like NCAA wrestling, but they were all science experiments. There's still a bunch of that left in our sport—and, at the lower levels, the tests are a joke. It's only at the highest levels where real steroid testing happens, and, even then, guys get by. The difference between PED's in our sport and in a sport like baseball is pretty major—if a guy doubles his strength, he's not hitting a ball farther than he would have ordinarily hit it, he's smashing someone's brain harder than he would have.

"You're right, it's not fair. And you're probably right about the drugs also, but you have to ask yourself what you want to do here. The light heavyweight title is vacant now that Wes moved on to the UFC. The number two contender behind you is injured, and that leaves you and Jason as the next two in line. I convinced John to make it a title fight if you agree to take it."

"Convinced? Why did you have to convince him? It seems pretty logical to me."

"Lucas, you got knocked out. Cold. Ranking barely matters at this point. It's a hard sell to get a guy who just lost his last fight in brutal fashion to step right back into a title fight. But I did it because it's what you want. But, if you say yes, then Jason is the guy. I have to call John back. What am I telling him?"

I don't know what I want to do—on one hand this is my shot—a chance to erase my last loss and get right back in the game for a chance to maybe get signed to the UFC. On the other hand, nothing is guaranteed even if I win, especially since they signed Wes. On top of that, I have to fight a guy who's dirty, who I already have a loss to. Fuck, this game is unforgiving. I need to think.

Before I can do that, Jackie, our manager, knocks on Matt's office door. "Lucas, someone's at the desk asking for you. Said she needs to talk to you."

"She?" I ask. "Who is it?"

"No idea. Says her name is Mila and that she's a student of yours. You want me to tell her you're busy?"

"No!" I yell. "Tell her I'll be right out."

Look at this shit. She came back. Now that I'm not lying in bed, horny and thinking of her hot body, I'm not so sure I really want to see her. The feelings I had when she stormed out yesterday come back, and I'm annoyed again. I was already kind of pissed at how this conversation with Matt was going, but now all I can remember is her being bitchy and running out like a little kid after dealing me that verbal low blow. I can't wait to see her, and to give her a piece of my mind.

"Lucas, be nice, alright. I didn't tell you about her situation, but you have to be gentle with her."

I jump up, annoyed, and ready to look her in the face and tell her what I think of her. Matt's words aren't going to deter me. He's usually pretty good at helping me keep my hot headedness in check, but right now I'm like that bratty high school kid who just told his math teacher where he can stick his homework assignment.

"Don't care right now, Matt, all due respect. No story or situation is going to explain being rude like she was. Tell

John I'll take the fight. I want an eight-week camp, non-negotiable, and I want extra drug testing."

"I'm not sure we're in a position to make those kinds of demands, but I'll try."

"Work your magic, Master Splinter—make it happen!"

I storm out of his office, not sure what I'm really angry about anymore. It's impossible to separate cause from effect right now. I just feel like lashing out at someone.

I storm into the lobby and see her standing there at the desk, looking fine as hell. As soon as my eyes hit her, my anger takes a back seat to my attraction. In the short walk from Matt's office to the front, I had a few things planned out that I wanted to say to her, but now that I'm laying eyes on her all I see is how fucking hot she is, and I forget all about what happened yesterday—mostly.

"Well, look who it is? Didn't think I'd be seeing you again."

"Hey." She looks different in real clothes. Yesterday she was in work out gear—tights, a tee shirt, and her hair was tied back in a bun. Now she's wearing tight fitting jeans, a nice shirt, and her hair is down, swooped over to one side of her neck. That gets me every time. She looks amazing, and I'm pretty sure that I'm staring at her. "Can I talk to you?"

"I thought I'd be the last person you wanted to talk to again."

"Yeah," she says. "That's kind of what I wanted to talk to you about."

"You want to talk to me about not talking to me?"

"Sort of. I mean, not really. Do you have anything for the next hour? Like a lesson or a class?"

"He's free as a bird!" I turn around to the sound of Matt's voice. "I'm covering his class today, don't worry.

Lucas is going to be doing fewer classes anyhow, he's got a fight coming up and training camp starts tomorrow."

I smile. Leave it to Matt to get things done.

"No shit? Thanks, man."

"You got it, champ. Now go. I've got things locked down here. Tomorrow we get to work."

"Indeed, we will."

There's a scene in Rocky II that reminds me of what I'm feeling right now. It's right after Rocky and Adrian have their baby, and he's sitting next to her bed in the hospital. The whole movie he's been talking about a rematch with the champion—Apollo Creed—and for the whole movie Adrian shut him down. Finally, when Rocky gives in and agrees to get a regular job, Adrian pulls him in and tells him to fight Apollo, but on one condition. *Win*, she says to him, *win*. The look on his face is pure joy, total surprise, followed by a hunger to go and prove that he's the better fighter. That's how I feel right now.

"Listen," Mila says, pulling my attention back to her. "I was a little rude to you yesterday."

"A little?"

"Jeez, you're not going to make this easy on me, are you?"

"Nope," I say with a smile. "Not at all." She swallows hard. I can tell she isn't the type to apologize much. The idea of it seems to be making her physically uncomfortable.

"Well, okay then. Maybe this was a bad idea."

She looks down and starts to walk away again. I stop her right away by putting my hand on her shoulder. I don't even think about it, my arm just reaches out instinctually to stop her, like it was meant to touch her in that moment. I stop her and she jerks around.

"Wait. No. I'm sorry, I'm being a dick. What did you want to say?"

"Are you hungry?" she asks.

"Huh?"

"It's a simple question. Are. You. Hungry?"

"Ummm. . . sure."

"Great. I know a place. Let's go."

CHAPTER TWELVE

MILA

It's easy to forget how tall Lucas is. Not just tall—he's a big man in all ways. When he was training me it was easy to forget that. You know what they say—lying down, we're all the same size. But standing next to him is a different thing—standing, we're not the same size at all. He's a mountain, casting a shadow over me, and making me feel safe for no reason whatsoever. It's been forever since I've felt that.

For months now, men have inspired the opposite feelings in me—apprehension, fear, anxiety. But Lucas doesn't do that. He makes those feelings go away, and I'm not sure exactly why that is. His size is one thing, and the fact that he's very good looking is another. Couple that with the fact that he's a fighter, and you have a person who might be the first guy to make me feel protected in a very long time.

My plan was to show up, apologize for being rude, and just maybe talk to him about taking another self-defense lesson. Now, I'm heading off to eat with this ruggedly handsome guy who I was fighting with twenty-four hours ago.

We get to a diner around the corner from his gym. I've never been here—I saw it on the way to my lesson when Holly drove me in—but clearly Lucas has been here before. As soon as we walk in they give him a hero's welcome.

"Yo, champ!"

"Stop calling me that, Spiro. Or at least save it until I actually am."

The older, very Greek man standing behind the lunch counter smiles. "What's that American expression? Fake it until it's true?"

"That's 'fake it until you make it', Spiro, but good try."

"Eh, I can't keep up with all the sayings in this country."

"You don't give yourself enough credit," Lucas jokes. "You're doing a great job."

The hostess sits us in a booth right by the entrance. The whole time we were walking over here I was thinking about what to say to him—how to apologize properly, how to tell him that I want to keep taking lessons from him. But the thought that's really dominating everything in my brain right now is how hot he is. Even the hostess—a young blonde girl who clearly knows Lucas—was giving him the eye. He didn't react at all—maybe he's used to being looked at that way by women, but I noticed it.

"Come here a lot?" I ask.

"Once or twice," he tells me before motioning at the booth. "Sit."

I do. And practically as soon as my butt hits the seat I try to apologize, only he speaks first. "Don't worry about yesterday. It's nothing. It may have caught me off guard and pissed me off when you said it, but I don't hold grudges."

It's the last thing I'm expecting him to say. I was literally rehearsing my apology to him on my drive over but I guess it wasn't necessary. "Really? Are you su. . ."

"You were rude, and so was I. I wasn't having a best day. Shit happens, we move on. No hard feelings, okay?"

And just like that the drama of our first meeting is gone, and I feel stupid for stressing about it in the first place. "Wow," I say.

"What?"

"Nothing, I just wasn't expecting you to be so cool about the whole thing."

"Mila, I'm a fighter. I get punched in the face for a living. Grown men try to strangle me on a regular basis. So, no offense, but nothing you can say to me at the gym is going to hurt my feelings for long, don't worry."

I guess he's right. I know that he's an MMA fighter—I saw what happened to him in his last fight. It may have been a little silly to think that my attitude would really do much to him. But still, I feel bad that he may have gotten the wrong impression of me. Hopefully today can make up for it.

"How'd you get into it?" I ask. "Did you come from a bad background?" I regret asking that as soon as the words leave my mouth, but he doesn't get offended, he just snickers at me. "Stupid question, huh?"

"It's not the first time someone's asked me that, so don't feel bad."

"Is that your way of saying that it *is* a stupid question?"

"Kind of," he laughs. "I didn't want to come out and just say that, but, yeah."

"I'm sorry." He leans in towards me across the table that separates us. At first, I don't know what he's doing, and instinctually I lean back and flinch. He looks at me sideways and puts his back against the back of the booth again, as if not to scare me. It's moments like this that remind me I'm not all the way mentally healed yet. Now I'm embarrassed. "Sorry, again."

"Listen," he says. "You need to do me a favor and stop apologizing. I didn't mean to scare you, but that's what I was going to say. Stop apologizing. You won't hurt my feelings, I promise."

He's been trying to put me at east this entire time, but I realize that I'm not at ease. I'm tense, my shoulders are sore, and now I feel like my cheeks might be turning red from embarrassment. "I. . . I'm not going to apologize again because you just told me not to, but can I explain something?"

"Yeah, of course."

"You didn't scare me. I mean, you scare me a little— you're really big and muscular. . ." *Stop talking, Mila. Just shut the fuck up before you really embarrass yourself!* "I'm saying all the wrong stuff. Maybe I should just go. . ."

I stand, abruptly. He doesn't get up or do anything dramatic. All he says is, "You ever try box breathing?"

It's a weird response to what I just did, but weird breaks me out of my own mind for a second. "Huh?"

"It's a simple question. Have you ever tried box breathing?"

"What's that?" I ask. A waiter starts to come over but Lucas puts his hand up with such quiet authority as if to tell the guy that this isn't the time. He walks away. Lucas looks right back at me, never getting worked up at the crazy girl standing across from him.

"You're having bad anxiety right now. I can see it all over you. I'm not an anxious person, but it happens to me pretty bad right before a fight. Matt introduced me to this

breathing technique called 'box breathing' and ⌐
works. It's when you breathe in for a certain amount ○
hold your breath, then let it out for a set time also. You
repeat it a few times until your anxiety goes away."

"And that works?" I ask.

"It helps," he tells me. "Look, it's not going to cure you
of feeling anxious completely, but it'll take the edge off.
Like popping a Tylenol for a bad headache. It's something.
Can I show you?" he asks.

I realize when he asks me that, I'm still standing. I was
fully ready to rush out of the place like a lunatic, but I sit
back down and try to maintain the kind of eye contact that
he's making. His look is really intense, and it freaks me out
and intrigues me at the same time. I'm not even sure what
I'm feeing anymore, but I know that I really don't want to
leave. "Of course."

"Do you mind?" he asks holding his arms out over the
table. He wants me to take his hand, and the fact that he's
asking me makes me calm down. I don't answer him in
words—I just put my hands into his. The first thing I notice
is how big they are—and how I expect them to be rough,
even though they're not. He holds on to me and never looks
away, almost like we're not sitting in a public place, but like
we're alone somewhere together. He's giving me the kind of
intense attention that's off putting at first, but once I get
used to it my heart starts racing in a good way.

"So, what do we do now that we're holding hands at this
diner?" I smile but he doesn't, just keeps on looking at me.

"Watch me. Do what I do. Inhale for seven, hold for
five, exhale for eight. We're going to do that four times. Like
this."

He does the entire thing with me, four times in a row,
exaggerating his inhales and exhales for my benefit. By the

second time, I feel my heart slowing, and I feel my whole body calming down because of it. By the fourth time I'm totally relaxed, and I don't remember why I was so nervous in the first place.

"Wow. That's a nifty little trick. Who showed you that, again?"

"My trainer, Matt. I call him Master Splinter."

"Like the Ninja Turtles?" I ask. He smiles when I do.

"Yeah, exactly. He's just like that wise old rat. Knows all sorts of crazy shit, but all of it works. If he tells me to do something, I just do it, no questions asked."

"You get it also? Anxiety, I mean."

"Just before a fight. Right before. When I'm in the back getting my hands taped and am warming up. Otherwise I'm as calm and collected as a person gets. And once the fight starts all of it leaves me, and I'm totally relaxed."

"Relaxed? The words 'fight' and 'relaxed' don't really go together, do they?"

"Maybe not for most people," he says. "But for me they're one in the same. Maybe relaxation isn't the right word—it's more like a sense of total calm. It's just like when you've been meditating for a while."

Mediation? This guy surprises me with everything he says. "You meditate?"

"Every night. My mind isn't right without it. Helps me keep this calm all the time."

"Okay, we'll revisit that, because you might be one of the most interesting guys I've met in a long time, but back to the fighting thing for a second. How is fighting like meditating? If I knew I had to fight someone, I'd be shaking uncontrollably and trying to run out of the cage."

He laughs. It's a deep belly laugh, and it's such a great sound. I don't take offense at all even though he is technically laughing at me. "I don't think it would be career move for me to do that, but trust me, I felt like it or twice when I first started out."

"But still, how can you be calm when you know that you could seriously get hurt?"

He thinks about my question. Really thinks about it—almost like he's never quite had to articulate the answer he's about to give me before. "It's hard to explain, but to me fighting isn't about violence or being violent. I know that's hard to understand if you don't do it."

"A little," I say. "You are using violence."

"That's true, I'm not going to deny it. Fighting *is* violence, but I guess what I'm saying is that the violence is a byproduct to me. I don't train every day and put my health at risk because I want to hurt people. I don't want to hurt anyone, and I sure as fuck don't want to be hurt myself."

Listening to him is fascinating. Not only is what he's saying something I've never even considered, but I'm also lost in his eyes—sitting this close to him I can see the deep blue of them—so deep it's almost hard to tell that they're blue at all. His face is relaxed but those eyes are always intense—always with a fire burning just behind them, and every so often I stop listening to his words and just lose myself.

"So, if that's true, then why fight? What is it that makes you go to train everyday if it isn't the danger and violence of it all?"

"To me, a fight is a metaphor—it's symbolic of the struggles that we all go through every day, only it's a more condensed version that lasts a few minutes. A fight is about testing yourself—seeing who you really are when faced with the ultimate kind of adversity. It's the purest form of self-expression that there is, and its problem solving with dire consequences. I love it all—the rush of knowing what it means if you make even one mistake; the struggle to stay motivated; the battle against yourself when your body and mind want to do nothing but quit. I love it all. The violence is just a side effect of all of that."

It's hard to impress me, and even harder to challenge my ideas, but Lucas just did both. I have to be honest—I always thought that fighting was a dumb man's activity — I wouldn't have called it a sport even though everyone else does—but now I'm seeing that there are layers to it that I never considered before. That's how I'm starting to see Lucas—as a man with layers. Interesting.

"You just blew my mind, you know that?"

"I'm glad. I like to surprise people in any way that I can. And by the way, I didn't come from a bad background. My parents have been married twenty-five years, I grew up middle class, and up until a few years ago I had a regular job while I trained. I'm nuts—all fighters are in one way or another—but I'm not some fucked up kid from the wrong side of the tracks, if that's what you were thinking."

"Kind of, yeah. I'm sorry for stereotyping you before. And even though you said not to apologize, I'm sorry that I was rude to you. You didn't deserve that."

"'In the sun, in the sun I feel as one.'"

"Huh?"

"Nirvana," he says. "All Apologies. You saying sorry about eighty times just reminded me of that song. My mind makes weird connections sometimes."

"Which do you like better, the original or the MTV Unplugged version?"

"Look at you! Maybe I'm not the only one who can surprise people. I've made two pop culture references in a short time and you caught them both. I love it."

"Why thank you."

This whole thing is unexpected. I love the way it's going, but I'm also starting to realize something that I didn't want to admit to myself the first time I saw Lucas—I'm attracted to him. I felt it the first time, but I wouldn't let myself really feel it. Since the incident, I haven't allowed myself a lot of feelings, especially towards guys, but sitting here with him, having a good time and listening to him, I think he's fucking hot. And not only do I want him to keep talking, I want to touch him again.

Lucas waves the waiter back over and we order our food finally. A short time later, the waiter drops off our food and we start eating, our meal punctuated by amazing conversation. We talk while we eat—mostly me asking more fighting questions, but avoiding anything about his last fight or him getting knocked out. I hit a sore spot last time when I threw that in his face, and it's not something I want to revisit just yet and take the chance of ruining the nice moment we're having. Instead, he asks me a question as our meal is winding down.

"Can I ask you something? You don't have to answer it if you're not comfortable."

My heart starts to beat a little faster—not like before, but faster than normal because I think I know what he's going to ask me. But he's been really open with me, so I'm going to be open with him. "Ask away."

"Before our lesson, Matt told me that you were a special case—that you'd been through some stuff. He didn't tell me anything more than that, but I was curious what that was. You don't have to tell me if you don't want to."

I don't want to. I don't want to tell anyone. *Not you, not even my therapist, but there's something about the way you look at me that makes me want to tell you everything—to give you everything that you ask me for. I can't deny it any longer. It's time to start opening myself up again. But not just yet.* I lean forward, just like he did before, and give him the kind of intense eye contact and attention that he's been giving me the whole time. That's when I decide to be as bold as he is when he steps into that octagon.

"I'll make you a deal."

"A deal?" he asks, raising his eyebrows up and smiling. "What kind of deal?"

"I'll tell you all about it, but not here."

"Where, then?"

"Tomorrow night, when you take me to dinner. I'll tell you then."

"When I take you. . . oh." He stops. He looks genuinely shocked, like he didn't expect me to say that to him. I love it. "It's a deal. Go easy on me, okay?"

"Never," I joke. "You're tough. You can take whatever I have to give."

"Should I wear my cup?" he jokes.

If it were up to me, Lucas, you wouldn't be wearing anything.

"Nope," I tell him. "I won't do anything below the belt that you don't want me to."

CHAPTER THIRTEEN

LUCAS

I'm finally falling asleep. It's the first time in a long time that I've slipped so soundly away from the chaos and stress of my day. As I close my eyes there's only one thing going through my mind—Mila. It doesn't make sense. I should be thinking of other things, like the upcoming fight that could change my life forever. Those are the things that normally run through my mind when I'm alone at night.

Tonight though, it's only her.

No gym stuff, no career concerns, no stress whatsoever. Instead, those things are replaced by a dream—or maybe a memory—of this afternoon. It starts the same—her asking me to take her to dinner tomorrow night, and me almost shitting my pants at what this hot woman was saying. At first, I was shocked, then happy, then a little worried about dating someone right as I'm about to go into the most important training camp of my life.

But I could not say no to her. No fucking way. No chance.

When it really happened, I gladly accepted, told her

how surprised I was, and left a few minutes after that with a promise to see her tomorrow night.

But dreams aren't reality—there are no rules when I dream, and I prefer no rules.

In my dream version of our encounter, we don't leave separately. I take her by the hand and bring her to my car. She gets in, not a word spoken between us, and we drive back to my place. There's no communication along the way except for her putting her left hand high up on my leg, close to the rapidly developing hard-on that's making my pants feel a little tighter than they are.

Next, we're inside—and, once we are, she loses all inhibitions—she's not the timid, scared woman who first spoke to me during lunch at the diner, she's a hell cat—a confident, sexy ass woman who knows what she wants. And what she wants is me. Once the door to my apartment closes, she's all over me, and I'm all over her. It's hard to even tell who initiates what—it's more like two bodies smashing against one another in the most passionate way possible. Individual sensations disappear, and they're replaced by an intense feeling of wanting to be inside of her at all costs. My cock is rock hard, pushing into my pants, and she claws against my back as we kiss mercilessly.

I grab the back of her hair and pull her back, just to let her know that I'm in control of her body. She doesn't fight me—she lets me take control and pull her head back just enough so that our lips are an inch apart. I can smell the sweetness of her breath, and she's trying to lean into me again, but I hold her in place until I'm ready. With my other hand, I reach underneath her dress and tease the outside of her pussy with my middle finger. She's soaking wet. I can feel her drenched panties just sitting there, getting in my way, so I move my finger around the side until I feel nothing but the warm wetness of her, and that's when I tickle her clit.

She gasps as I make contact, moving my finger in small, strong circles. Her body collapses, and I let go of her hair because she isn't fighting me anymore. Now she's mine, taking all the pleasure I'm giving to her, letting me control her body and mind like I'm supposed to. I reach down even lower, and slide my finger as deep inside of her as it will go. I feel her whole body tighten as I go in, sliding in and out, and using my thumb to encircle her clit as I do.

I wake up, drenched in sweat. It's a feeling I'm used to after I've done two hours of training at the gym, but not one I usually experience at one a.m. in my own bed—at least not alone! But when I look at the clock, reality hits me and I realize two things—first, training camp for my title fight starts today, and I need to get some fucking sleep. And two, tonight I have a date with Mila!

The next eight weeks is going to be interesting.

CHAPTER FOURTEEN

LUCAS

Training camps suck. No way around it, and anyone who tells you different is a liar.

They're the grind of all grinds—requiring discipline on a level most people aren't capable of.

I grab a large coffee and make the drive to the gym. He's waiting for me when I walk in ten minutes past when we agreed. He looks like the principal of a high school, tapping his watch and giving me the judgmental eye like I need to get the fuck to science class, asap.

"I think my watch must be fast because I have 9:10."

"Don't be a dick," I say, feeling a little grumpy from the lack of sleep and the caffeine not quite doing enough to make up for it.

"Don't be late. Conduct yourself like the champion you want to be."

Training camp changes everyone, including Matt. He becomes less like Master Splinter and more like General Patton—a task master who gives no fucks about excuses or personal issues unless they're extreme enough to warrant interrupting our goals. Sleeping badly doesn't meet that criteria.

"I'm sorry, you're right."

"I know I'm right. And Lucas, camp is twelve weeks this time around," Matt says.

"Twelve? I said I wanted an eight-week camp!" I yell, my frustration getting the better of me.

"I know you said eight, but twelve is what you're getting. You took a hard hit and were knocked out cold, Lucas. You may think you're ready, but you haven't trained hard for a fight in over a year. I don't want you to push too hard too fast and blow this shot."

I know he's right and I box breathe to get my temper back in check before I say something stupid. I look at Matt and he has a look in his eye daring me to challenge him. I don't.

"Is George here yet?"

"George has been here for almost an hour. He got here ahead of time to change and warm up. Let's not waste his time, he's doing this as a favor to you. He could be making a lot of money doing seminars the next few weeks."

"Shit. Alright, I'll go change, give me five."

"Three. And no more."

I run and throw my Gi on in the back. George is one of my best training partners—a true stud. He's not a fighter himself, but he's one of the best Jiu Jitsu players on planet Earth. The guy submits everyone, including in the open weight division, which is for anyone, no matter how big or small. First time I saw him was on a YouTube clip where he choked out a guy who outweighed him by fifty pounds at least. I bring him in whenever I need to work on my grappling, and what's even crazier is that he does this for free.

That's what no one realizes about training camps and fighters—we have to pay for everything. We pay our coaches, our training partners, everyone. But I don't make enough on my fights to do that, so I developed some great relationships with top guys who fly out and help me for free if I agree to do the same for them for their fights.

As I get changed, I hear my phone ring in my bag. I stop dressing for a second, even though all I need to do is tie my belt, just to see who it is. When I see a number and not a name I actually know that it's Mila. It's a text, and all it says is, "Looking forward to tonight. Thanks for lunch yesterday." That part is cool enough, but the blushing smile emoji at the end is what I really notice.

I decide to not mention any of this to Matt—he has a thing with instructors dating or messing around with anyone who comes to our gym. It's a big no-no, and even though Mila isn't really a student per say, it's still not somewhere I want to go with Matt—especially when he's in training camp mode and his sense of humor dies a little more each day. I text her back with my own emoji, then hit the mats.

George is looking like a killer—the kid is only twenty-four and has a murderous look on his face at all times. He's actually a really cool guy, but on the mat, I don't want a cool guy, I want a trained assassin who's trying to submit me every chance he gets. That's the only way I'll get better, and there's no way I'm losing this fight to that roid head. Not only do I need to get that loss back, but I'm also fighting for clean fighters everywhere. The icing on the cake—the thing I can't afford to think about yet, is my career after I win. I want that meeting that Wes had with Sean. I want the call up. I want to be in the UFC.

But first, I have to train... hard.

Today starts my journey.

Let's do this.

CHAPTER FIFTEEN

MILA

Holly comes over my apartment with a bottle of wine.

I think it's bad when your friends have too strong of an association of you with something like alcohol—they think that you drink day and night, and that's only partially true. I actually haven't touched the stuff since the last time all us girls went out together. Since my Jiu Jitsu lesson with Lucas, I haven't even thought of taking a drink, but that's mostly because I have't thought about Brett. No memories of waking up in the hospital, or of having my orbital bone broken so badly that the surgeon told me it was one of the worst cases he'd seen in over twenty years of practicing medicine, and no memories of how long it took me to even get up enough courage to live on my own again.

Six months doesn't sound like a lot of time, and really it isn't. It's less than a school year. It's about the length of a hockey season. It's no time at all, except for when you're trying to mentally and physically recover from almost being killed. Then, six months is a lifetime—the time it takes to develop a new version of you—one that isn't a scared little girl who can't do anything with her friends and family. Holly and Sophie were both things to me. You know what they say? That it's only in the bad times that we see who our real friends are. Well I went through the worst time imaginable, and my girls were everything to me. There through thick and thin—mostly thick—and there to support me even when I needed them less and less as the months went on.

Holly, in particular. She was my rock. And it's her who I need to talk to right now.

"You need to move into a building with an elevator, I swear. No more of this sixth-floor walk-up bullshit."

"Listen to yourself," I joke. "You're in the best shape of anyone I know. You ran the friggin' Boston Marathon two years ago!"

"Yeah, yeah," she jokes. "It's not the same, though. There's just something about having to walk up stairs that always sucks."

"And you think I'm the complex one?" I smile and she smiles back. Holly and I have known each other since we were kids. We grew up together in Queens and met at P.S. 104 when we were in the second grade. We've been best friends ever since. We both met Sophie the next year, in third grade, when her family moved into the neighborhood from New Jersey. Now we all live in the city, about a train stop or two away from each other.

"You are. Hey, when are you going back?"

"Back to?"

"Your job," Holly says. "The kids have to miss you."

"Oh. Right."

The kids. It was always my dream to be a teacher, and I fulfilled that dream after college. I was lucky enough to get a job right away teaching second grade at an elementary school in Brooklyn.

"Probably not this year," I tell her. "Actually, no 'probably' —I can't go back this school year, I'm not ready."

"I'm so sorry, Mila. Didn't mean to touch a nerve, I didn't know."

"It's okay. I wish I had a different answer."

"I know."

I obviously had to take a leave after the assault, and despite all the other handicaps that came from what happened, one of the hardest was having to leave my job. The kids really help make my life what it is. I'm one of those teachers who truly loves what they do. I didn't take the job for a paycheck, or because I get a few months off in the summer. I took it because I love giving the little ones the best experience they can have. But the truth is that they enrich my life as much as I try to enrich theirs.

"On a happier note, I think we need to have a talk about our fighter friend. Spill all the tea."

"There's no tea. We're just... having a meal."

"You're having a second meal! That's two meals in two days—tell me you're banging an MMA fighter?"

"Jesus, Holly, no one is banging anyone. We're just having dinner."

"Okay, just dinner." I can hear the sarcasm dripping off her words. "But can I ask you one question?"

"Sure."

"Did you shave your legs today?"

"You're too much."

"So, is that a yes?"

"No," I tell her. "For your information, I didn't."

"Are you going to do it later?"

She's got me. "Maybe," I say coyly. I can't help but grin. She catches it right away.

"Holy crap. You like Lucas. You're gonna marry him and have a million little fighter babies."

"Shut up!"

"I know you better than almost anyone in the world, Mila, and I haven't seen that grin on your face in years. You like him, admit it."

I do like him. How much, and what that even means is something I haven't decided for myself yet. I'm not sure how much I'm ready to get into this yet. "Of course I like him, he's a nice guy."

"Nice? You're giving me nice? Who do you think he is, the old lady in the apartment across the way who gives out whole Snickers bars to the kids on Halloween? She's *nice*. You don't describe someone as hot and dangerous as Lucas as 'nice.'"

Dangerous. I've never thought of him that way. But I guess he is. I mean, he hurts people for a living, and he gets hurt in return. I know he explained the whole violence thing to me, and it all made sense, but regardless, he's still like a human weapon if he wants to be, and part of me is really scared by that—but also really excited.

"What's wrong with being nice? It's a nice thing to say about a person, isn't it?"

"Listen to yourself, girl. You've used that word more than I have in the last year. Guys you want to fuck aren't 'nice'—you can describe them any other way, but not that way. So, is he just a nice martial artist you want to have a nice meal with and talk Jiu Jitsu, or is he a hot instructor you want to bang?"

"Ummm. . . is there an in between?"

"Between a guy you want to fuck and a guy you don't?

No, sweetie, there's no in between for that—it's one or the other. Yes or no. Left or right."

"Hmmm, interesting. If those are my only two choices. . ." I drag out the end of my sentence just to mess with her a little. I can see she's hanging on my every word.

"Yeah?"

"Then I'd have to say 'yes.'"

"I knew it!!! Yes!!!"

"Relax," I tell her. "He is still someone I want to have a meal with, and saying that I just want to fuck him makes it sound so. . . shallow."

"Shallow is fine. Look, I know better than anyone how traumatized you were, and I'm not trying to make light of your recovery, or to push you into something you're not ready for."

"I appreciate that."

"But. . ."

"How did I know there'd be a but?"

"Cause you're psychic," she jokes. "But I'm your friend, not your therapist, and that means I'm going to take a different approach than someone licensed by the state who you see once a week. They get paid to see you and, no matter how many times you go there, your doctor will never know what you've been through the way I have."

"I agree with all that. So, what's your prescription, then?"

"I think that you've come back from the kind of experience that would break most women, and despite the fact that you still get anxious, and that you haven't thought of any guy the way you're clearly thinking of our cage fighting friend, that it's okay that you pursue an opportunity when it comes along. You're a strong woman, Mila—one of the strongest I know, and you deserve to feel normal again.

So, when you meet a hot guy and you want to see how far it will go, I say go for it. Why not?"

Why not is right? Yeah, I still have some issues—more than some—but I can't just sit in my apartment all day waiting to feel like my old self before I decide to start living again. I needed to hear her say what I was already thinking all along—I deserve this.

"This is why we're sisters," I tell her. "You tell me the truth when I need it the most."

"And I always will. And so will Sophie."

"I love you guys so much."

"We love you too," she tells me. "And that's why you need to never refer to Lucas as 'nice' in my presence again—I don't care if the man reads to blind children on the weekends. In public, call him by his name—and to me, he's Lucas the Fuck Buddy Esparza. That's his new fight name."

"You're the worst, Holly."

"I know," she jokes. "That's why you love me."

"It is. It really is."

CHAPTER SIXTEEN

LUCAS

There are a few expressions in fighting that everyone who fights knows—tried and true sayings that you forget until they happen to you, and then you remember their particular wisdom. I just experienced one.

You win, or you learn.

Losing is for losers, in other words. Either you win a competition, or you learn what you need to do better for next time. I just got a hard reminder of that in training. George submitted me ten times. But that's not what I'll remember. I'll remember that I need to work my offensive guard a little more; that I need to control my opponents posture better—I'll remember the little things my coach always tells me that I never listen to.

After George played with me on the mat I did some hard cardio and waited for Matt "the Second" to come by. I told Master Splinter that I wanted to keep working with the kid even though I was in camp. He still has big issues at school, and I don't want to abandon him now. I remember what that's like.

When I was getting shit at school, I told only two people—my science teacher, Mr. O'Brien, and my guidance counsellor, Mr. Mackey. O'Brien was one of those teachers who wanted to be cool with his students, so he basically told me that I was exaggerating when I told him what some of the guys were saying and doing to me. He didn't go so far as to call me a liar, but that's exactly how he made me feel. Mackey was another story—that guy was a dick—the type of adult who should have never been put in a position to help kids with their problems. He did all but call me a pussy. Told me to stop complaining, and that maybe if I was more 'social', I wouldn't have been made fun of so much. I'll never forget how betrayed I felt, and the last thing I want to do is treat Matt's problems like my teachers did to me.

After waiting around for about ten minutes Matt calls me over. "What's up?" I ask.

"Kid cancelled. You have your afternoon free."

"Cancelled?" I ask. "Did he say why?"

"Nope. Dad wouldn't say—just that the kid had a bad experience at school or something, and that he didn't feel like coming in."

Bad experience? That's usually code for 'other kids gave me more shit than I can handle'—I hope it wasn't anything too serious, the kid was just starting to gain some self-confidence.

"Shit. I hope he's good."

"How's he doing with you?"

"Good," I tell Matt. "We didn't drill any techniques yet or anything—been working some self-defense fundamentals with him—like good posture, eye contact, and how he carries himself. That, and we just started some fitness stuff."

"That all sounds good. I'm sure he'll be back."

"Yeah, I hope so."

Soon as I know I have some time to myself I get changed and head off to the sauna to sweat a little bit. The intense heat always makes me feel better after a hard workout, and today was pretty fucking hard. I guess I should suck it up—this is only the beginning.

An hour later I get out of the sauna, sweating from places that I didn't even know existed on my body. Afterwards I take a shower and check my phone before heading out of the gym. There's nothing new from Mila, but I start to think about what's happening later on. There are a few cool new restaurants around, but I have no idea what she likes. Plus, she probably knows about them already. I start to think, then I have an idea and decide to text it to her.

Me: Hey. Don't know if you're comfortable with this, but, if you want, how about I cook something for you?

I'm kind of nervous sending that text, and I have no idea how comfortable she's going to be going on a first date at my place. Maybe it was stupid to even. . .

Mila: I love the idea. Didn't take you for a cook.

Me: I'm full of surprises. It's not weird to come to my place?

Mila: How about we have sex right away to get the awkwardness out of the way. Then maybe a glass of wine.

I read that line about five times, faster than I've ever read anything in my entire life. I'm deciding whether or not to ask if she's serious when she sends the laughing face emoji. I send one back.

Me: I'm not going to argue with you there. I

kind of assumed sex, wine, then dinner. As long as we get to all three, the order doesn't matter.

Mila: Agreed.

I like this girl. I never thought I'd say that after our first encounter, but she's really cool—has a great sense of humor, willing to apologize when she was wrong, and what's most important—hot as shit! For real, her body and face are something out of a movie, and she doesn't seem to even be aware of it. Some girls are stuck up—completely conscious of the fact that they're beautiful, but if Mila knows how gorgeous she is then she isn't showing it at all. I like it. I can't wait to see her later.

Now I just have to figure out what the hell I'm cooking.

CHAPTER SEVENTEEN

MILA

Legs shaved, dress on, bottle of my favorite wine ready to go. With my checklist all done, I head out to drive over to Lucas' place. Maybe I'm crazy going over to a guy's place when I barely know him, but I felt a connection the other day, then felt it again at lunch, that I want to explore. Part of me feels normal—like a woman who wants to be with an attractive man—and the other part of me still feels like Brett's victim, afraid to do anything without a full-fledged panic attack ensuing. But I tell that bitch to shut up and pretend to act like the woman I want to be—I'll fake it until I make it.

When I get to his place I ring the bell and get suddenly nervous. Not only am I going to his place, but he's cooking a meal for me, which is super hot. A man who can kick ass and cook is a rare thing, and yet another stereotype I had in my head gets destroyed. I'm actually excited to be out doing something instead of sitting in my apartment watching TV.

I hear his footsteps approach and my heart starts racing, in a good way. When the door opens, I hardly recognize him. To say that the boy cleans up nicely would be the understatement of the century. He's dressed to the nines in a nice pair of black khakis and a white button down. The shirt is tight enough to outline all the muscles of his chest perfectly, and I catch myself staring a little.

"You look beautiful," he says.

If I blushed, I'd be blushing now. I do my awkward smile thing instead. "Thank you. You look great too. I'm not used to seeing you outside of in a gi."

"I do own other clothes. I have a closet and everything."

"I'll believe it when I see it."

He laughs and invites me in. His place is nice—small and a little messy, like I'd expect of a young guy who lives alone, but the smell of something delicious is filling the air.

"Did you find the place okay?"

"Uh-huh. What the hell did we do before GPS was invented?"

"Learn how to figure things out, I think, but I barely remember that. You didn't have to bring the wine, I have some."

"So, my friends think I'm a wine-o, which I'm totally not, but I am very particular as to what I like and what I don't."

"Okay, red or white? Let's start with the basics."

"Red, always."

"I have red," he says. "But what kind?"

"Guess my favorite kind."

"Oh, I'm no good at that. You think I know all the different types of red wine?"

"C'mon, you have to know at least one. Try."

"Merlot?"

"Good job. But not my favorite."

"Ummm. . . Cabernet is one, right?"

"It is, and I like a good Cab, but not what I brought with me."

"I'm tapping out," he jokes. "It'll be the first time doing that in a while, but I have no idea of any other red wines. Tell me." I pull the bottle out from behind my back and hold it out for him to see. "What the fuck is Shiraz?"

"It's an Australian red. This one isn't too dry."

"Oh good," he says, being more than a little sarcastic. "I hate when wet things are too dry. That sucks."

"Shut up."

I try not to make it obvious that I'm checking out what's on the menu. I look over his shoulder into the kitchen while he uncorks the wine and see he has a big pot ready to boil pasta, and I smell some amazing aromas coming from the oven. He catches me looking everything over as he starts pouring us each a glass.

"Pasta primavera," he tells me. "But I'm not having the pasta. I have some grilled chicken cut up in the fridge to go with the veggies."

"How come?" I ask. "It smells delicious."

"Thank you. And fight camp. I'm not quite cutting weight yet, but I'm still on a strict diet. Basically, no refined carbs until after the fight. I'll have them at my celebration dinner."

"Can I ask a stupid question?"

"There are no stupid questions."

"You haven't heard mine yet. What does it mean to cut weight?"

"That's not a dumb question at all, by the way. And it involves watching what I eat, but eventually I'll be losing a lot of weight closer to the fight to get down to the weight I fight at, which is 205 pounds."

"What do weigh right now?"

"240, so it's not that much weight to lose."

"240! Holy crap, that's actually a crazy amount of weight to lose. Why don't you fight at a different weight then?"

"Size and strength advantage. But it sucks to cut weight —it's basically getting rid of water in your body so you shed pounds really fast, but then you gain it all back right after."

"That sounds not fun at all."

He smiles. "It sucks worse than I could explain. Be happy that you don't know what it's like. I'm not there yet, though, but I do need to watch my diet so I don't balloon up and have to cut even more weight."

"I see, so you'll feed me all the fattening food but you're not going to eat any yourself. I see how it is."

"Trust me I'd love some carbs right now, but I know I'll pay for it later. I read a social media post recently that said no food tastes as good as victory—I try to remind myself of that so I stay disciplined."

"And what about the wine? Can you drink when you're training?"

"Nope," he says. "But I'll have one sip and leave the rest to you."

"So, let me get this straight—I'm going to get drunk and eat all the heavy food while you eat veggies and drink water."

"Basically, yeah."

"Got it, just checking."

We spend the next few minutes getting to know each other even more as the pasta boils. I offer to help him set the table but he refuses and does everything for me. Brett wasn't anything like this—none of my exes were—even before the incident. Brett never did anything like cook for me. I'm not used to a guy paying such close attention to everything that

I say or taking care of things the way Lucas is doing. There's a contradiction in him that's making me so turned on—he's a tough guy—someone I've watched on YouTube dishing out an ass whooping to other giants, yet I never feel like I'm with someone like that when I'm around him.

"Do you like talking about it?" I ask. "Fighting, I mean."

"I like talking about whatever you want to ask me about."

"Nice answer," I joke. "But seriously, we can talk about other things. You probably have fighting on your mind 24/7, so I don't want to force you to talk about it."

"It's true, I think about the fight game a lot—not just the actual fighting, but also my training, my career, the sport in general. Shit, I even come home and watch fights on UFC Fight Pass."

"What's that?"

"It's an app where the UFC has all of their old fights and shows archived. You pay monthly, like Netflix, and you can watch all the fights you want. It's pretty cool."

"And you don't get sick of it? I think the last thing I'd want to do after training like you do all day is come home and watch guys fight in a cage."

He laughs. I can tell that he isn't so into the topic, but he's entertaining my curiosity. "Some guys are like that, but I love it so much. I can't get enough. I'm as much of a fan as I am a fighter."

"Really?" I ask. "That's interesting. I always thought. . ."

"That people who fight have to fight because they have no other options?"

The man's a mind reader. Or maybe I'm just that transparent. Maybe both. I practically turn red when I hear him say it—it sounds so stereotypical and ignorant to hear, but it is what I've always thought. "Yeah, kinda," I admit.

"Don't feel bad." He reaches across the table and touches me on the hand. His touch is fire—electricity running through my entire body, and when he quickly pulls away I feel cold. "A lot of people think that, and it's actually true for a lot of guys, especially old school boxers. But now it's different—people go into MMA like they go into amateur wrestling—it's a sport, and people of all different backgrounds take part in it. A lot of fighters actually have college degrees, small businesses, and are from backgrounds that you wouldn't expect."

"Huh. I hate to say it, but that surprises me."

"How come?" he asks.

"I don't know. I guess I can't really understand why someone who could be making a lot of money in an office somewhere would willingly choose to get hit and choked out in front of crowds of people."

"Yeah, I get that. It's hard to explain."

"Can you try? I'm curious."

I really am. It's so weird because I never thought I'd be interested in something like cage fighting. I grew up with a dad who watched baseball and football. There was never a boxing match on the TV, and I had all these preconceived notions about fighters and fighting. But now that I've met Lucas—now that I'm listening to him—I really find every aspect of this sport really interesting.

"Yeah, I can try." He does that thing again where he thinks really hard. I can see that he's trying to put the right words together so that someone like me can understand the world he lives and trains in every day.

"Fighting is for people who like challenges, but not challenges like in a math class. It's for people who want to figure out just who they are, and how good they are at something." He stops, almost like he's not happy with what he's saying. I can see the frustration on his face. "I'm doing a shit job here."

"No," I say, reaching over the table and touching his hand like he touched mine, only I leave it there and look him in the eyes. "Keep going, you're doing fine. What kind of challenges?"

"We all lie to ourselves in some way, right? We tell ourself a narrative about who we are and what we can do. Sometimes it's honest but a lot of times it's just what we tell ourselves so that we feel better about who we are. Do you know what I mean?"

I sure do, I think. *More than you know.* "Uh-huh."

"Well, fighting is the purest no-bullshit zone that exists. Inside the octagon—or even at the gym—you can't lie to yourself. You can't fool yourself. Narratives don't matter because who you are is on display right there, for you and everyone else to see."

"Like, how?"

"In every single way. If you're a coward it shows. If you didn't put in the hard work to learn a technique or get your cardio where it needs to be, it'll show. If you think you're tough but you really aren't, it'll show."

"Oh, I get it now. But is it a positive thing? You make it sound like it just shows you who you're not."

"Oh no," he says. "It does that too, but it shows you who you really are, whether you want to admit it or not. And if you're not the person you thought, then you can either quit, or get better until you actually are that person. I'm in the second category."

Hearing him talk like this is doing something more than just interesting me in what he does for a living. I didn't really understand at first, but the more he talks to me—the more he looks at me with that intense glare and talks about what fighting means to him, the more attracted to him I feel. Not just attracted. The more I want him.

I try not to let it show on my face, but it's the parts of me he can't see that are really feeling him—I feel a tingle between my legs, something I haven't felt in a long time, and as I'm listening to him talk about personal challenges, I also imagine what his body would feel like on top of me.

"That's amazing," I say, mostly to distract from how I'm probably looking at him. "I get it, it's just hard to imagine actually doing that for a living."

"It's hard for me, too, sometimes." He laughs at his own joke, and it's cute. "But my dream—what I really want to do, is make it into the UFC."

Even I know those three letters. The UFC is the biggest MMA organization in the world, and I had no idea that he had these kinds of ambitions—yet another thing that makes him attractive to me.

"The UFC? That's incredible. Do you. . . I mean. . . not sure how to ask this, but. . ."

"Am I good enough?"

"You really have to stop finishing my sentences—it's freaking me out a little."

"Sorry, but was I right?"

"Maybe." I can't help but crack a smile on that one. He really knows what I'm thinking each time.

"Here's what I can tell you. Remember when I just said that this sport teaches you who you really are? Well, I know that I'm good enough to compete with the guys in the UFC —but I need to prove it to a few people who really matter. That's what my next fight is all about."

"Oh, I see. And that's why that knockout was so bad?" I regret it right as I say it. I was going out of my way to avoid bringing up that sore subject again, but I just let my mouth get in front of my mind. I really didn't mean anything by it. "Shit, I'm sorry."

"No, let's talk about it. I'm actually glad you brought it up." Glad? That's the last thing I thought he'd be.

"Are you sure?"

"Yeah, it's fine. Relax, I can see how tense you are right now. I'm not going to bite, it's okay."

Biting seems like a great idea right now. Fuck, I need to stop!

"As long as you're okay talking about it. I didn't exactly bring it up in the best way."

"No, it's okay, I promise." He stops and looks at me so intensely that I feel like he's looking right into my soul. His voice is deep, and every inch of his face looks like it's been chiseled from pure granite. "And you can ask me anything you want. I'll always tell you the truth."

I just fucking melted.

"Okay. So, tell me, how disappointed were you?"

"That's really hard to put into words. Imagine something you worked for for months—a singular purpose that you put all of your time, money, and effort into. Now imagine feeling great, feeling prepared, doing all of the right things, except for one small mistake that ruined everything. That's how it felt. I disappointed myself, but even worse, I feel like I let my entire team down. It's the worst feeling in the world."

"I'm so sorry. I really am. That sounds heartbreaking."

"That's exactly what it was. Not just because of the loss. I do hate to lose, but I can deal with that. It's more that I felt like I let everyone down—all the people who believed in me and put their blood, sweat and tears into making me this war machine. And on top of that, the guy who beat me got a deal with the UFC—he posted on his Twitter recently.

He got a three-fight deal that should have been mine, if only I'd held my hands up higher to block that shot."

He exhales deeply. That's a lot to let out on a first date, but I feel so honored that he trusted me with something that's still obviously painful to him. "I know you're going to make it one day. I realize I don't know you that well yet, but you have a great attitude, and you said that you're only one fight away, right?"

"I don't actually know, but I think so. If I can beat Jason, and do it in spectacular fashion, I think that I'll impress the right people and get that deal. It's all I've ever dreamed about."

"Then you'll do it. I know you will."

I don't know that. I don't know it at all. But I believe in him, and more than anything else I want to take that frustrated look off of his face and never have it return.

"Thank you. I really appreciate that. Now, can I ask you a question?"

"Anything."

"Why did you come to take self-defense classes? I meant to ask you."

"How come?" I ask. I know it sounds defensive, and I don't mean it to, but he threw me off guard with that question. I don't know why, I should have expected it at some point, but I got so caught up in our discussion of him and his career that I forgot about me for a while there. Now I have to decide how to handle this.

"I always like to know why my students take lessons," he goes on. "It doesn't matter to me at all, I just like to know, and you never told me. I've been telling you all about me, which I don't mind, but I feel like an arrogant asshole talking about myself all night. I want to know about you too."

What the hell do I do here? I don't want to lie to him—I know that, but I'm also not sure that telling him that I was almost killed by my ex is something that I want to get into right now. It's not a simple thing—it's a long, complicated thing that has about a million follow up questions that I'll have to answer. I decide to go with a half truth, and hope that's enough for now.

"I was. . . I was attacked about a year ago. Some guy robbed me when I was coming home alone. He beat me up and I was in the hospital for a while. It was bad."

I look down as I tell him, but when I look back up I'm taken aback by the look he's giving me. He looks so concerned that I almost start crying. His brow is furrowed, and he's looking at me with gentle eyes.

"What? Why didn't you tell me that at the gym?"

"I don't know," I tell him. "I was in a bad space when I met you—I didn't really want to be there. I thought the whole thing was stupid. I'm sorry."

"Don't apologize, you were a victim. I'm so sorry you got hurt. You said about a year ago?"

"Yeah. I had some pretty bad injuries. It was touch and go for a while. The recovery was worse than the attack."

"Did they catch the guy? Tell me that motherfucker's rotting in a prison cell right now."

"They caught him. He's in prison, but he only got a few years." I feel like shit leaving out the most important detail of this story. I tell myself it's not so bad because I'm mostly telling him the truth, but I still feel guilty.

"A few years? That piece of shit should rot away the rest of his miserable life in a cell."

He's worked up and I don't expect it. It frightens and excites me at the same time. His anger makes me nervous at first—a remnant from the attack—but the fact that it's in my defense, and that he's genuinely angry *for* me makes me want him even more than I did a few minutes ago.

"I know. The courts suck sometimes."

"Obviously. I'd love a few minutes alone with that guy, whoever he is. I'd take care of what our criminal justice system clearly couldn't."

"You don't just have to say that to make me feel better, you know?"

"I'm not," he says. "I don't do that. If I say something, I promise you that I mean it. I'd beat that man within an inch of his miserable life. I'm so sorry that happened to you."

"Thank you."

"Look, I know it's not my place to say this, but you're doing amazing. Really fucking impressive."

"Really?"

"Are you kidding me? You're stronger than half the fighters I know. You think it's easy coming back from something like that? It isn't. I've been beaten up, and I've been beaten unconscious, but I signed up for that risk, and it's something I do willingly because I love it. You got assaulted when you were just trying to walk home. That must have screwed up your head as much as it did your body."

You have no idea. No idea at all.

"Yeah. It did."

"I guess we make a good team, then. Two people who are a little screwed up from our recent experiences—only yours is way more serious than mine."

"I don't think you're screwed up. You'll be fine. You'll come back stronger than before."

"You, too, Mila. You even more than me. I know fighting, and I know fighters, and not every fight happens in a cage. The hardest ones happen in our living rooms, under the covers when no one's around, when we're dying inside but have to keep a smile on our faces. You're a fighter as much as I am—maybe even more so."

I can't explain what comes over me, but something does. It's uncontrollable—a wave of attraction crashes over my entire body, and I reach over and grab him by the collar of his shirt. The kiss is passionate and intense, and as we kiss we move away from the table and towards the couch. He tastes as good as he smells, and even though I've taken him off guard at first, he adjusts pretty damn quick. He grabs me by the hips and pulls me towards him. His grip is so strong it's almost intimidating. His hands are huge, and when he cups my body I feel like a doll in his grip. I press into him—into those hard muscles hiding just below his shirt, and I'm suddenly aware of how wet I am, how much I want him, and how right this all feels.

I don't hesitate, and I don't think about the past at all—I just act, slamming my body into his, and then. . .

CHAPTER EIGHTEEN

LUCAS

There used to be this old myth that sex during a training camp was bad luck—it was even a line in Rocky when Mickey said, '. . .women weaken legs.' The no sex thing is total bullshit, but old Mickey was a wise old man, because my normally steady legs are weak as hell right now. When Mila first started kissing me I didn't expect it at all, but I adjusted to that surprise pretty damn quick, let me tell you!

Now, I can tell she wants to do a lot more than just kissing. She's rubbing her hands all over my body, ripping at the buttons on my shirt like a rabid animal, and smashing her lips against mine violently. I'm not used to a woman being so sexually aggressive, and I definitely didn't expect it from her—but I'm fucking loving every second of this.

I can tell that she loves to kiss because she does it with uncontrolled passion. Her lips are warm, comforting, and she knows just how to use them. My cock is so hard that I don't know what to do with myself. She wants to make out, but all I can think of is fucking her uncontrollably. This kissing is only going to last so long. I wait a few more seconds, and in that time, she pushes her tongue into my mouth, making me even harder. It's not just my cock—it's my entire body, from my hair on the back of my neck down to my toes—all of it is turned on—all of it wants her. I've had enough.

I pull back and separate us, but only our mouths. I keep control over her body and start to undress her. I pull her shirt up, then her skirt down. Now she's standing in front of me in her bra and panties, her hair a total sexy mess, her cheeks red and flushed from how turned on she is. It's not just her face or her hot body standing in front of me that's driving me nuts, it's the crazy look in her eyes. She's looking at me like she hasn't eaten in a week and I'm a T-bone steak —like she wants to devour me—and that's exactly what I'm going to to let her do.

Her cheeks look like summer strawberries—rosy and beautiful, and I grab a hold of her face when she's right in front of me. I start to run my fingers through her hair, gripping it just enough to angle her head back. I'm about to lean in to devour her neck, but before I make it all the way in I hear her say, "Take your fucking pants off right now."

It's forceful and I love it. The woman knows what she wants, and I'm going to give it to her like she's never had it before. I unzip and pull my pants off. Then I pull my shirt over my head and throw it on the floor. What's left is me and my boxer briefs—black, the only color I own—with my hardness extending the fabric as far as it'll go without breaking. The sensation I'm feeling is something in between being totally turned on and being in pain. All I know is that the tension in my body is building, and it needs relief—fast.

She looks at me with those eyes—eyes filled with a burning passion. "Finish." That's all I need to hear. I pull my boxer briefs down and step out of them. She looks down, breaking eye contact for the first time since she grabbed my collar and kissed me. I know why she's staring, and she's not the first woman to give me that treatment. I'm not bragging, because I don't need to, but the truth is I've got a huge fucking dick. Right now, it's standing at full attention.

"Holy shit," she says, still holding her gaze on my throbbing member.

"Surprised?"

"A little. I mean. . . what do I even do with that?"

"I have a few ideas. Wanna see?"

This time it's my turn to take a forward step—two of them—until her firm tits are pushed up against me—the hardness of her nipples pressing into my chest through the thin fabric still covering them. I reach behind her and unclasp her bra. As the straps fall slowly down her arms I look at her beautiful breasts. They're perfect. Round, supple, and waiting to be in my hands and mouth. I lean over and start to suck on her nipple, and it's round and hard in my mouth. She moans, and runs her fingers passionately through my hair. I reach down with my other and squeeze her ass as hard as I can and she jumps. We start kissing again, but only for a few seconds.

The time for foreplay is over.

I scoop her up and carry her into my bedroom. She feels like nothing in my arms. Once we're inside I toss her onto the bed. She falls onto her back but sits up right away and grabs a hold of my cock. Before I know it, she takes me in her warm mouth. She closes her lips and then I feel the suction as she moves her mouth methodically up and down my shaft, pulling gently at the base as she does. I feel like I'm all the way down her throat, and she takes every single inch of me, and that's no small task. I can't help but grab her hair and pull her forward. She let's me, and I hold her there, my cock replacing whatever space she has in my mouth and throat. While I hold her, she grabs my ass with both hands and runs her nails against my skin. When I let go she goes back to work, moving backwards and forwards quickly, then slowly, until my eyes are rolling in the back of my head.

When she's done sucking my cock, I push her down by the shoulders and inch my way onto the bed. She opens her legs wide for me, and lies on her back in a totally submissive posture that's driving me absolutely fucking insane. I take a second to look at her—how hot she is, how sexy her body is just lying there waiting to be defiled by me. My eyes take in all that they can. Now it's time for our bodies to go to work.

I'm so hard that it hurts, and there's only one thing that's going to relieve the force that's building like a pressure cooker ready to erupt, and it's sitting between her legs, staring at me. She sits up and we start kissing, and while we are I reach down and put my middle finger as deep inside of her as it will go. She's so tight! Once I'm in her I move in and out, and reach up with my thumb and circle her clit with as much pressure as she can take. As soon as I hit that spot her whole body reacts like she just got an electric shock. I keep going, separating from our kiss and priming her pussy for what's about to come.

She strokes my cock as I finger her, but there's no need. I've never been this rock hard in my life, and when I feel the wetness covering my entire hand I know it's time. I grab myself, covering my dick in all of her juices. She's going to need to be wet to take all of me inside her. I position the head of my red swollen cock right on the lips of her pussy and we make eye contact. I like to tease. I rub the outside with my head, and tap her clit a few times until she's ready to go.

She grabs onto my wrists. "Put that huge cock in me right fucking now."

"You want all of this?"

"Give it to me, baby. I want every fucking inch right now!"

"Be careful what you wish for."

I thrust forward, guiding myself with my hands at first, then letting my hips do all the work. With a single push I hear her moan, and her eyes open wide like she just saw a ghost. I can tell she's never had something this big inside of her before, and she's loving it.

"Oh my fucking God, Lucas!"

"That's right. And now I'm going to fuck you."

"You'd better—fuck me right now!"

I grab onto her hips as she angles her whole pelvis up towards me. I'm on my knees, and I start fucking her silly. Not only can I tell that she's never been fucked by someone this big, I can tell she's never had a man go this hard or this deep. Her whole body is shaking. Her eyes are closed and her mouth is open, so I put a finger inside of it as I fuck her, and she latches on and sucks it hard. It doesn't stop my rhythm, it just makes me go even harder.

"Don't fucking stop!" she yells. I have no intention of stopping. I make sure to pull all the way out before reinserting myself, so that she gets the full breadth of my hard, swollen manhood. After a minute, I turn her over and tease the outside of her ass. I'm destroying that little pink pussy. I spread her open with one hand as she balances on all fours. I slide inside so easily and grab her hips again and start pumping. Her body is slamming into mine, and the slapping sound is echoing throughout the room.

I want to keep going, but the sight of her and the feeling of her tight, wet pussy is making me want to come all over her, right now. "Are you ready for this come? I want to give it all to you."

"Shoot it all over me, baby, give me all of it."

I'm there. I pull out just when it feels like I can't take anymore. I'm out of her just as I start to spasm. She turns over and I shoot a hot load of thick white cum all over her tits. Some of it goes even higher, touching her neck. She lies there and takes it, a huge smile on her face as I explode everywhere. "Oh, fuck!" I yell as the last drops fall onto her sweaty body. Then I let myself go. But it's not over.

I dive down and spread her legs open. It's time to let my tongue go to work. I know this isn't going to take long at all. I start to rub my tongue all over her clit, finger-fucking her as I do. She starts to shake and moan right away.

"Oh, fuck, I'm gonna come again. . . holy shit, Lucas!" If her body seemed like it got a shock before when I first touched her clit, now it's trembling like she's got a thousand volts running through her all at once. Her pussy clenches around my finger, and I keep working until she collapses. When it's over we lie there, sweaty, happy, and—quite frankly—still a little turned on. "I've never come that hard in my entire life. Holy crap."

I wrap my arm around her and she puts her head on my chest.

I don't say it, but I've never come that hard either. I've never experienced anything quite like that before. I don't know what it is, but there's just something about this girl!

CHAPTER NINETEEN

LUCAS

The Next Day

"Keep your hands up, bitch!"

The shit talking follows a stiff jab to my nose. My life is so fucking weird.

Last night all I felt was pleasure—the feeling of her soft skin and tight body against mine. Hours and hours of some of the best sex I've ever had. It seemed like it went on forever, and I loved every second of it. And now I'm feeling different things against my skin—mostly leather.

The dude screaming at me is Mike Suranov —a Russian lightweight amateur boxer who has a real chance of making the Olympic team next time the games come around. His real name is Mikhail, but we all just call him Mike around here. The kid's hands are lighting, and if you're not on your game he'll piece you up in there. Even with head gear and a venti Starbucks coffee coursing through my veins I'm still struggling with my reaction time. Oh yeah, and he also loves to talk crazy shit when he spars.

"If we were in prison, I'd make you my bitch. You know that, right?"

He says the whackiest shit just to motivate his training partners whenever he feels like they're not giving their all. Apparently today he's attacking my body and my masculinity. It's all good, though—Mike's a cool dude, and to be honest I need a little motivation. It's not that my head's not in the game—my head's always in the game—it's just that it's early in fight camp, and I'm still not in fight shape. But really, it's last night. I'd never tell Matt what happened because he's old school about stuff like that, but I am a little too relaxed.

I get my back off the ropes and use my footwork to get back to the center of the ring. I hit Mike with two left jabs, a right cross, and a left uppercut in a rapid-fire succession. Then I decide to talk some shit of my own. "Who'd be the bitch again?" I hit him some more. "Not me." I get a second wind and unload a barrage of punches and duck all of his counters.

The bell rings to signify time is up, and I drop my arms and then tap gloves with Mike. "Good shit." His English is broken. He's still a Russian citizen, traveling back and forth between New York and Dagestan in between fights—but he trains here a few times a year, and always flies in when I have a camp. He's one of my best training partners.

"Good shit indeed."

I don't get changed because I have Matt "the Second" coming in for another workout. After sparring, Master Splinter calls me over. "You look good, but your reaction time is off. He got the better of you a few times in there and you're a better boxer than that."

He's right. I got it back at the end of our round, but I'm way better than that. Mike's a better boxer than I am, by far, but he doesn't usually get the better of me for that long in a sparring session. Maybe Mila's making me soft. Nah, I just need to get my head into fight camp mode.

"You know how I am at the start of training camps."

"I do," he tells me. "But I also remember what happened last time. Do I really need to remind you about everything?"

I don't mean to dip my head down like I'm embarrassed, it just happens. "No," I say, ashamed. "No, you don't."

Master Splinter's honesty hits harder than any fighter I've ever met. It's what I love and hate about him, but to be fair the hate part is just because I don't like to be reminded of my own mistakes. There was a lot of shit that went down in my last training camp before the fight with Wes. Matt's not a petty guy, but he will remind me in a not-so-subtle way when he feels I need it. He's just looking out for my best interest, but it still stings.

"Good." He puts his hand on my shoulder, almost like a dad. "Listen, I've been around fighters my whole life. Self-sabotage is a real thing. Sometimes we say that we want something, but then our actions tell a different story. I've been around this game long enough to know not to trust people's words—I just see how they're behaving. You remember last time. Now I need you to have your shit together if you really want what you say you want."

"Yes, sir. I get it. I'll do better next time."

"That's all I needed to hear. Oh, the kid will be here soon for his lesson today. Just a heads up, his dad sounded a little urgent on the phone."

"What the hell's going on with that?"

"No idea, but it's something. Guy sounded upset. Just watch out, he might come in hot."

"I can handle hot, don't worry."

About thirty minutes later Matt the Second walks in with his dad. Before he even gets to me I have the whole situation figured out. Dad looks like he's ready to kill someone, and Matt has one of the worst black eyes I've seen in a long time, and I've seen a lot of them.

"What the hell kind of operation are you people running here?" Nothing like an angry father. He's irrational, and his face is turning red. Of course he's upset, his kid keeps getting his ass whipped, I get it. My dad looked the same way when it was me.

"Sir. . ."

Master Splinter tries to jump in, but I put my hand up to let him know that I've got the situation under control. These kinds of things don't bother me at all. "He got beat up?" I ask.

"Yes! He got beat up. Again! I thought you were teaching him self-defense."

"Dad, I. . ."

"Quiet, Matthew!" his father yells. "Let me handle this."

"I have an idea," I say. Steven stops and looks at me. "How about we let Matthew tell me what happened before we start screaming and blaming anyone? Because I'd like to know what the situation was exactly."

First Steven just gives me the crazy eyes. I meet them with quiet confidence, and he slowly meets my energy level. He strikes me as the kind of guy who gets what he wants by yelling and being intimidating. Corporate type. But I fight trained killers for a living, so some red face and crazy eyes don't bother me any. Finally, he concedes.

"Fine. Matthew, explain please."

"It was in gym class," he begins. "The same two kids who always mess with me started doing it again. I did what you said, professor. I kept my shoulders back the whole day, I looked people in the eye. I did all of that."

"Okay. That's all good, it's what I told you to do. So what happened next?"

"I looked one of them in the eye and they took it like a challenge. 'What are you looking at, homo!'—that's what they yelled at me, in front of everyone."

"So, what did you do?" I ask.

"I didn't back down like I usually do. I didn't run away. I stood there with them, and when they tried to push me I swung at one of them, but I missed and the kid's friend sucker punched me and threw me to the ground. They each took turns hitting me until it got broken up. That's what happened. Just like that."

I'm sure that Matt's dad and I heard different stories, even though we heard the same story. What I mean to say is that I can already tell by the man's reaction that our *interpretations* of what Matt just said are totally different. What Matt's dad just heard is that he got into a fight and didn't know how to punch and kick, therefore it's our fault that he got beat up. But what I heard deserved a...

"Good for you, Matt. Atta boy."

"Excuse me? Did you just say 'good for you'?" I was expecting this reaction, so I turn all of my attention to Steven so that he can get the last of his bullshit out before I have a chance to rebut. "What is wrong with you people? Have you taken one too many blows to the head or something?"

"Dad!"

"Quiet, Matthew. Listen, I'm paying you..."

"For your son to learn self defense, correct?"

"Yes, and clearly you don't know what you're doing if

this is still happening to him. I've had enough of this already!"

The man practically has tears of frustration in his eyes. I'm not taking a single word he's saying personally, because I remember my dad's anger and feeling of helplessness when he saw me getting harassed all the time at school. I don't have a kid yet, but I can't imagine what that's like.

"Steven, come over here and let's talk. Matthew, you come too. We'll use Master Splinter's office."

"Who?" Steven asks.

"Sorry. Matt, the gym owner. We'll use his office."

As understanding as I am of what Steven is feeling, I can't have the man make a bigger spectacle on the mats. There are people training, classes going on, and a general sense of balance. Last thing we need is a disgruntled parent throwing everything out of whack. Once we get into the back, I sit in Matt's seat and motion for Steven and Matt to sit on the other side. I don't give him time to talk, I just start to explain the situation from my point of view.

"Sir, listen. . ."

"Steven, please."

"Fine, Steven, then. I want you to understand something that only a few people in the world know about me, okay?" Steven nods. "I was bullied before bullying was a word everyone knew. For me it was the 8th grade. Every day was hell. It got so bad that I used to find reasons not to go to school—I'd have sudden illnesses so often that my parents started taking me to specialists."

"Jesus," Steven says. I can tell his face and tone have softened since his outburst. Now he looks less angry, and more like the concerned parent who walked his son through the front doors of the gym to begin with. "That must have been hell on your parents."

"It was. Just like this is for you. I can't imagine. But I need you to see things the right way in order for you to help Matthew as much as you can."

"And what way is that?" he asks.

"Not like a father. I know that's a huge thing to ask, but you have to try to separate the emotion from this. Yes, Matthew got into an altercation that he probably shouldn't have. And yes, he got hit, which definitely shouldn't have happened. And if I were you, I'd speak to that school. . ."

"Already done. My law firm is contacting the superintended to put the fear of God in them."

I like Steven even more now. "Good," I say, smiling. "I'm glad to hear that. But the hard truth is that you can't litigate or create policies to get rid of kids being dicks to one another—pardon my language."

"Please," Steven says. "We're all men here."

"That we are. So, look, let me be straight with you—with the both of you. When you walked in here the first time, your boy needed instruction to even look at me for more than two seconds. He was hunched over, looked insecure, and was a walking victim. That's the truth. And now, he's fixed his posture, he's looking people in the eye, and he tried to defend himself physically. It doesn't matter that he got beat up—he stood up to those kids, and that makes all the difference in the world when it comes to bullies."

"I didn't think of it like that."

"I know. But that's why we're in this room. Even though things look the same to you, they aren't. He's growing. He's gaining confidence. He swung back. Matt, have you ever thrown a punch at anyone who's bothered you before?"

"Never. I don't really know how to."

"That's okay," I tell him. "I'll show you. I'll show you

everything you need for next time, if there is a next time. But first, you had to take the most important step alone—and that's standing up to those fuckers."

"Thank you," Steven says. "I'm sorry, I overreacted out there. I apologize."

"Never apologize for defending your boy. I'd expect nothing less. This will end one day, I promise you that."

"I hope so," he says. "I really do."

Matthew sits up in his chair and looks at me with more confidence than I've seen from him since we met. "So, what do we learn next?"

I smile. I can't help it. I'm a devious fuck. "Now, Matt "the Second"? Now, I show you the good stuff."

CHAPTER TWENTY

MILA

I'm sick of therapy.

I know I should be thankful to have such a good psychologist in my life as Dr. Chase has been to me, but I'm honestly sick of going. I feel like therapy should be something finite—a tool you use to get better and then you're done. I don't want to be one of those people who get stuck in some doctor's office year after year, complaining about their lives and looking for answers from the other side of the table. I want to find my own answers, and I feel like I'm finally getting there.

Dr. Chase has been a godsend, really. My family helped me find one of the best trauma psychologists in New York because I was in no position to do research when I first got out of the hospital. I'm lucky that I come from a well-educated family because they knew that my mind would still be screwed up long after my body healed, and they were right. I had all the symptoms of PTSD—anxiety attacks, changes in personality, I was quick to anger, and scared for no reason. Luckily, Dr. Chase works primarily with battered women and combat vets—people who, frankly, have gone through worse than I did, so he knew how to help me.

After our early afternoon session, I decide to meet up with Sophie and Holly for a later lunch. They both work close to my doctor's office in the city, and I thought what better way to kill an hour than with my best friends—and this time I have some things I want them to hear about. We meet at a local café.

"Hey girl!"

Sophie is so loud, but I love her for it. "Hey. Thanks for meeting me."

"Anything to get out of the office," Holly says.

"Gee, thanks. And here I thought you'd want to spend some time with me."

"We do. Don't listen to this skank." Holly gives Sophie the middle finger, and we all laugh.

"So?" she asks. "How was your session?"

"It was good, I guess. I mean, as good as therapy gets, if 'good' is a thing when it comes to dealing with your issues."

"There are bad therapy sessions, believe me."

Sophie knows of what she speaks. She's the fun loving one of the bunch—always silly, and always up for a good time, but she experienced some real trauma herself when she was younger, and she's worked her ass off to get to the level of stability she's at now.

"Yeah," I say. "I know. I've had a few, but nothing crazy. Today was good. We started talking about an exit strategy."

"From therapy?" Holly asks.

I nod. "Yeah. It's been almost a year of sessions. At first it was three or four times a week, now it's down to one. I feel like eventually we should hit zero. Maybe I'm just being impatient, but I feel like I'm getting past the point where I need to see someone."

"How are your symptoms?"

Sophie can go from silly to serious really fast, and sometimes it's hard to keep up. But when it comes to topics like this she's all business. She's gotten her life together, has a great guy she's been seeing, and has a really good job. But it wasn't always like that. Now that she's back on her feet, she looks after me like a mom. They both do. I love them for it, but sometimes I just want to interact with them normally.

"Better," I tell them. "Much better. I still get some anxiety leaving the house, but I'm getting better at dealing with it."

"That's great news," Holly tells me. "You seem better. But maybe there are other reasons for that besides therapy, huh?"

She gives me the look—the I-know-something-is-up look that only a girlfriend can give you. Sophie catches it. "What? Did I miss something?"

"Why don't you ask our girl here," Holly says. "I'm dying to know myself."

"Well???" Sophie asks. "Spill the beans, girl."

I'm not the kiss-and-tell sort, but it's been such a rough road to get towards something resembling normalcy that I'm actually really psyched to tell my best friends what happened. So psyched, that I forget we're in public and I blurt out. . .

"I fucked him, and he has such a huge dick!"

The second I say it, I want to die. Not figuratively. Literally. I want to crawl up into my embarrassed self and disappear, only I can't stop laughing hysterically, and neither can Sophie. We make such a spectacle that everyone around is looking at us, and I'm not sure if it's because we're laughing a little too loud, or because I just yelled out 'huge dick' in public. Either way it's not a good look.

"Holy shit, Mila, tell us how you really feel."

"I don't know what just came over me. I'm sorry."

"Sorry?" Sophie asks. "Never apologize for appreciating a nice big dick. Good for you!"

"I think we need to go," Holly says. "We're getting a few 'those-girls-are-talking-dicks' stares from everyone. Not sure I can keep on talking about it here, but I need details."

"Me, too."

"Alright, let's get out of here," I tell them. "I'll tell you all about Lucas."

CHAPTER TWENTY-ONE

LUCAS

I basically live in the gym when I'm training.

I'm here so much that sometimes I don't leave. Depending on when my sessions are and when my training partners come by, I make this place like my home. There's a cot in Matt's office where I grab a nap sometimes. There's a mini fridge where I keep all of my meal-prepped lunches and snacks, and there's a locker and shower. It's pretty much my house at this point, and my house could use a deep fucking cleaning.

Gyms basically smell like shit. There are worse smells, for sure, and I'm used to the funk of sweaty dudes and mats, but this place could use a cleaning. When I was a kid that's how I paid for my membership. I was in high school at the time, and no one wanted me to have to get a job on top of school and learning how to defend myself. My parents could have afforded lessons, but back then it was all about teaching me lessons—so, like someone who has to wash his dishes in order to eat at a restaurant, I cleaned the gym so that I could train. I'd wash towels, clean the mats, clean the ring, organize the gear, and when I got better I was a free training partner for the guys getting ready for a fight.

This gym has a history. It was originally owned by Matt's father, Gregory, back in the day. He trained Matt before MMA was even a thing—back then it was a kickboxing, karate, and wrestling gym where the general public could come and take lessons, but where the real fighters trained after all the classes had ended. Matt was a great fighter in a time when great fighters didn't have a lot of options. He made it pretty far on the amateur kickboxing circuit, and later he got really into Brazilian Jiu Jitsu, but he got a bad injury that sidelined him, and that's when he became a trainer. I've seen footage of his fights—and I think he's an even better coach than he was a fighter. After his dad died, Matt took over the gym, and he's trained a lot of guys whose names you'd know if I told you. Their pictures cover the walls of the gym.

Tonight, I'm all alone, though. I have a key and Matt knows I enjoy the occasional late-night solo workout to clear my head, so here I am.

I did two sessions today, and I'm starting to feel like I'm getting into fight shape. When your average person talks about getting into shape, they mean that they're going to lose a few pounds, or maybe gain a few in muscle mass, or just tone up their body so they look good in the summer when they're laying out on a beach somewhere. Fight shape is a whole different thing—that kind of shape takes weeks to get into, and it's training your body to go anywhere from fifteen to twenty-five minutes, full force, with another grown man trying to take your head off. I'm not nearly there yet, but I'm starting to feel less exhausted with each workout.

I decide to stay behind and move around a little. I'm feeling stressed about the fight. I'd never admit that to anyone, but I'm still haunted by memories of my fight with Wes. Up to that point I'd never been knocked out, and that loss shook my confidence. On the other hand, I met this amazing woman, and when I've been with her over the last few days I forget all of my problems. I forget about being woken up that night with smelling salts and doctor's lights shining in my eyes. When I was with her I didn't think about how sore my arms are, or how many times I took a jab to the face in sparring. When I'm with her, all I think about is her—Mila.

I need to text her. I go into my bag and get my phone out. Before I can text her, I see that I have a text from her. It's from a half hour ago.

Mila: Hey. What are you doing? I had a very embarrassing moment today involving you lol. Love to tell you about it.

It's 10:00 pm now, and the text is time stamped at 9:35. I text her back right away because she's been on my mind ever since our amazing night together. I really want to see her again.

Me: Hey. Sorry I missed this. Are you still around?

Mila: I am. Where are you?

Me: Where I always am.

Mila: Gym???

Me: Where else. Wanna come by?

Mila: Like for a lesson, lol.

Me: Like, just to hang out. I'm here alone. Place is closed and everyone's gone home.

Mila: Give me an hour.

Me: Alright. Text me when you're here, I'll unlock door.

The last couple weeks with Mila have been some of the best that I can remember. Just being around her is almost as exhilarating as a win after a fight—almost. I don't even realize it's happened, but I get rock hard at the thought of her. Literally, my dick feels like pure bone hitting against the front of my shorts. Thank God no one's around or I'd be fucking embarrassed. But no one's around except me—and soon Mila. That girl has a crazy effect on my body and mind. Just by reading her text, I start to picture her naked body—tight and thin, just like last night—her hair gripped in my hand as I. . .

Shit, I have to stop. I can't have the girl walk in while I have a giant hard on. *Think of baseball, think of baseball, think of anything but her tight little pussy. . .* fuck, this is harder than I thought! I try to redirect my mind from her body. Every time I try I just see her tits bouncing around as I rocked her entire body last night—as she looked up at me and let me put my finger in her mouth while I fucked her.

God, I have to think about something else. . . anything. . . I got it. I'm really into horror movies, and my favorite of all time is the original Texas Chainsaw Massacre from the 1970's. I start to think of the part where all the teens end up at Leatherface's house and see all the gross decomposing bodies. I close my eyes and think about a family of cannibals who skin people and make masks out of their skin—that's what it takes to get the image of Mila's hot body out of my mind. And it only lasts about ten seconds.

Only one thing's going to help.

I run into the back, throw my shorts on the ground, and jump in the coldest shower I've ever had in my life. I turn the 'C' dial as far right as that bitch will go, and throw my whole naked body right into the stream, dick first, until the shock of it kills that erection real fast. Cold water does the trick every time.

I get out of the shower after I've shocked my hard on into submission, then dry off real fast. I still wanted to get a little bit of a workout in before Mila gets here.

It is almost an hour to the minute before Mila texts me that she's parked out in front. I managed to get some shadow boxing and stretching in, but that's about it. Nothing heavy. The bag will have to wait until tomorrow. But I'm not thinking about my left hook when I hear my phone beep—my whole brain shifts to her, and I go to unlock the front.

"Hey there."

God, she looks amazing! She's standing in the doorway of the gym looking like pure sex. The breeze blows the smell of her hair into my nostrils and I breathe in deeply and give her a hug. "Hey yourself. You're right on time."

"I like to be punctual. I was actually early but I circled a few times in case you were busy. Didn't want to interrupt anything for your fight."

"Listen to me, you can interrupt me anytime you want. For real. Now come in."

"Yes, sir."

"Oooh," I joke. "I could get used to that 'sir' thing."

"Well be good to me and I might say it again tonight." I feel my dick start to harden when she says that and I make my way over to a bench to pretend I have a cramp in my foot. "Are you okay?"

"Yeah," I tell her, lying through my damn teeth. "I twisted my ankle a little sparring. Just stretching it, you know? Don't want to hurt it any more."

She knows I'm bullshitting—she can see it in my eyes. I just don't know if she knows *why* I'm bullshitting, but now isn't the time to mention it. Finally, I get a little more relaxed, at least enough to stand up without embarrassing myself.

As soon as I'm in the clear I stand up. I try to make some small talk to cover up the barely noticeable—but still there—bulge. "You know, I never asked you what you did for a living."

"I'm a teacher, actually. Elementary school."

Hearing that makes her even hotter to me. There's something about a woman who works with kids that's crazy attractive to me. And just cause I'm a devious fuck, Van Halley's 'Hot for Teacher' starts to play in my sick head. "That's incredible. How's the school year going?"

"I'm actually unemployed at the moment. Layoffs. I'm looking for a new job for next year."

"Oh shit, I'm sorry. That fuckin' sucks."

"It does, but I'm happy to have some free time to myself. Getting to 'do me' a little, you know? Get out of the grind, reflect."

"That's great. I wish I had time to do that. When you're a fighter, there's not a whole lot of time for much except fighting and training. Makes being in a relationship hard. Makes doing anything except fighting hard."

"Yeah, but you're dedicated. Most people don't have anywhere near the kind of discipline it takes to do a sport professionally. I admire that."

"Thank you," I tell her. I never thought I'd say this, but she really gets me. Gets me like not a lot of other girls have. Sure, I did the groupie thing early in my career—but those girls just like the idea of a guy who can fight, but they don't want to be in a relationship with a man who practically lives at the gym. Mila seems different than all the other girls I've known, and she legit is into the sport. "Wanna step into the ring we have?"

"For real?"

"For real, let's go."

She looks excited. She slips off her shoes and we step into the cage. She steps onto the canvas in front of me and bounces, almost losing her balance. I reach out my arm and grab her.

"The floor bounces more than I thought."

"Yeah it takes some getting used to." I'm holding her in place by the arm so that she can stabilize. It's just an excuse to put my hands on her, and I don't want to stop there. She doesn't try to stop me as I move my hands from her arm to her waist. She feels so good. The warmth of her body and the feeling of my hands on her has me hard as a rock again in no time. I grip her tightly, and she doesn't move or tell me to stop. Instead she reaches her head back towards me as I pull her ass into my hard cock. I can smell the sweetness of her hair as she leans, and we start to kiss right here in the cage.

I push myself into her so she can feel what she's doing to me. It's so hard that it hurts. It needs the relief of being inside of her right now. We kiss for a few seconds and then she turns her body so that she's facing me, and I grab her ass as hard as I can. When my hands slap against her cheeks she yells and we kiss again.

"It's so hard to keep your balance," she says.

"I'll hold you up."

"No, don't. Let me fall." She drops to her knees, pulling my shorts down with ease as she does. "I almost forgot how big it is. You think I can fit it all in my mouth?"

"I know you can."

"Hmmm," she says. "Let's see."

She swallows all of me—my throbbing manhood disappearing inside of her willing mouth. The warmth and suction of her feels amazing, and I push forward to make sure she's getting every last inch of me where it belongs. When she's done blowing me I follow her to the floor and take all of her clothes off. Her body is so amazing. I forget where we are and that anyone could pass by and see us if they were looking hard enough. I don't care. All my eyes will see is her. All my body will feel is what between her legs.

I slide inside her sweet pussy and we start to fuck. I push in deep, kissing her neck as I thrust in and out of her slowly. She's so wet that I fall out a few times and have to reposition myself. It's not a problem. I slide back in easily and hold her legs up straight in the air as I sit back and pound away at her pussy. The gym is silent except the noise of my balls hitting her ass as I shake her entire body.

"Fuck, that feels good!" she yells.

I keep at it until I'm sweating, the beads dripping down my chest. She reaches up and grabs at my pecs as I spread her legs open and bury myself as far as I can go inside of her. I reach down and start using my thumb to rub her clit. She moans uncontrollably. I can tell she's close, and so am I.

"I'm gonna come right now."

"Fuck, me too!"

I explode inside of her just as her body thrusts around like she's being electrocuted. I squeeze every last drop into her before we both collapse onto the canvas.

"That was amazing," I tell her, still breathing heavy. "But we should get out of here. Not a good look to be caught, naked, in the gym."

"True. How about my place?"

"Let's do it."

"How's your cardio?" she asks.

"For the fight?"

"Nope. For another few rounds with me?"

For that, I have a never-ending gas tank.

CHAPTER TWENTY-TWO

LUCAS

I've committed the cardinal sin of training camp.

I missed a session for no reason.

It wasn't because I needed rest, or because I hurt myself, it's because I wanted to spend time with Mila. I could have set my alarm after we got back to her place. Hell, I could have even slept at the gym. Even that would have been less suspicious than staying at her place and just no-showing to training. And it's not just a no-no, it's a big fucking no-no, especially for me.

When I open my eyes and look at the clock I roll my eyes. I hate the feeling of being in trouble because I'm a grown-ass man, but that's the rebellious side of me taking over. I realize that I have responsibilities to people other than myself once training for a fight starts. I have a nutritionist, sparring partners coming from all over the place, my striking coach, my head coach, and a few other people who all show up to help me be the best I can be.

Today was supposed to be another spar with Mike. The spar was supposed to be at eight. When I wake up and check my phone it says nine forty-five, and I know that I'm totally fucked.

Underneath the time are about ten messages from Matt and Mike, asking me where I am, asking if everything's okay, saying that they're worried about me because it's not like me to miss a training session once camp starts. I read them all, but I get the idea—I screwed this up, and now I have to face the music. I'm not going to text them back. This has to be more of a face-to-face thing.

She's not in the bed—I can hear her rustling around in the kitchen, and I can smell coffee like a Great White shark can sense blood in the ocean. She rounds the corner as I sit up. "Hey sleepy."

"Morning," I say through groggy eyes. "I didn't know what time it was. I missed practice."

"You go everyday, I'm sure it's okay if you miss one, right?"

It's moments like this when I remember that I don't have the same kind of job as other people. I'm not normal at all. My friends, my ex girlfriends, even my parents have asked the question she just asked before, and none of them get it. Ah, the fight game.

"It's whatever the opposite of okay is. Whatever that word is, that's what missing practice is."

"Oh," she says. "I didn't realize. I would have woken you up."

"Not your job. I'm a grown man. I should have set an alarm. I was a little. . . distracted."

"You sure were." She leans over and kisses me. The feeling of her lips first thing in the morning is something I could get used to. Her hair is down, and it's falling against the side of my face as we kiss. I feel everything in my body start to stiffen again. She's wearing nothing but a tee shirt, and I can't help but look down her shirt as she leans. Her tits are starting back at me, and she's over far enough that I can see the hint of her nipples, and my brain is fried all of a sudden. I force myself to look away.

"I really need to get out of here," I tell her. "Matt's going to fuckin' kill me. He sent me like six texts this morning."

"Is it really that big of a deal? Can't you just text him back and tell him that you overslept?"

I laugh. I don't mean to, but her suggestion is so ridiculous that my body just forces me to let out one of those sarcastic and obnoxious laughs. "You don't know Matt very well. That's the fighting equivalent of saying the dog at my homework. He has rules, and I just broke one."

"He has rules? What does that mean?"

I don't have the time to explain the ins and outs of fight camp or the fight game to her right now, but I stop to do the quick version so at least she doesn't think I'm making an excuse to leave here. Last thing I want is for her to think this has anything to do with her.

"Think of me and Matt having a relationship like a student and a master from one of those old karate movies from the 1970's."

"You think I've watched old karate movies from the 1970's? You're funny."

I smile. "Sorry. Umm. . . you ever see Kill Bill with Uma Thurman?"

"Oh yeah, I love Tarantino!"

Yes! I found a reference that'll work with her. "Perfect. You remember how Uma Thurman's character went to train with Pai Mei up in the mountains of Japan?"

"Oh yeah," she says. "Wait, Matt's like that? He hits you and stuff?"

"No, no. Matt doesn't hit me. It's not actually like that,

I'm just using a reference for you. He's not a dick like that old man, but he expects a certain level of respect from me, and he has a few cardinal rules that I never break."

"Sounds a little crazy," she says.

"Not crazy. Disciplined. To fight at a high level, you have to have the kind of dedication most people only dream of. That means being there every day, training your ass off. Missing days can throw off your whole shit."

I can see I'm losing her a little. It's stupid to explain to someone who doesn't live this life.

"Well, then you'd better get going, huh?" She leans over again when she says that. She knows exactly what she's doing, and it's working.

"Yeah, I'd better. But I don't want to."

"I don't want you to, either," she says.

It's too much. I'm a disciplined guy, but right now that discipline is going to complete shit, and at the moment I don't seem to care that much. I grab her by the arms and pull her forward on top of me and we start kissing. I'm gonna be in deep, deep shit with Matt. . . but, I'll deal with it later.

I don't want to go inside.

I sit in my car like a total pussy. I know what I'm going to see and hear when I get inside. Judgement. Yelling. Bullshit. None of which are going to help prepare me for my fight with Jason. But I have to face the music like a man.

It's one o'clock and I'm beyond late. My bag is next to me, and I grab it and walk through the front doors feeling bad. The first thing I do is scan the room for Matt. When I don't see him, I get a little concerned, because he's always either on the mats training with one of the guys, or he's behind the desk. Right now, he isn't in either place. Who I do see is Al, my striking coach. He's working with Jose—one of the up and coming kids in the gym.

"Al, you seen Matt anywhere?"

"Look who decided to show up? He's pissed with a capital P."

Here we go. "I know, I know. I wanted to talk to him. Have you seen him?"

"Yeah, kid. He worked with Mike since you didn't show up, and now they're both in the back. He said to send you back there when you finally showed up, if you did. So, I'd go back there and talk to him if I were you."

"Alright, thanks."

I feel like a kid being called down to the principal's office. I drop my bag in the front just off the mats and make the walk of shame into the back office. I open the door and Matt and Mike are sitting there, laughing it up and looking totally normal. Then Mike hears me walk in and the energy gets serious.

"Kid, where the fuck were you?" Mike's got that Russian I-don't-fuck-around vibe to him. He doesn't know how to mince words, and he doesn't pull any punches—literally and figuratively.

"I'm sorry. . . I fucked up, man. . ."

I don't even finish before Matt puts up his hand and dismisses Mike. "Would you mind leaving us alone, Mike? We need to talk."

"No problem, Coach."

On the way out, Mike gives me a cold fist bump, and I give it back. "Good luck," he whispers as he passes. It doesn't make me feel any better.

Matt looks pissed. I've known him long enough that I

can tell what he's feeling without him saying it, but I'm pretty sure he's going to say it anyhow. I sit down and brace myself for a lecture.

"I just have one question, Lucas. One, and only one, and I need you to answer me honestly, not with what you think I want to hear. Can you do that for me?"

"Yeah," I say. "Of course. What is it?"

"I need to know if you're willing to do what it takes to be a champion. That's not the same as asking if you want to be a champion, because everyone wants to be a champion. But I'm having serious doubts as to whether you're willing to put in what it takes to fulfill the dreams you say you have."

He did the parent thing with me—he didn't yell, and he doesn't start lecturing me. He pretty much did that thing where your dad tells you that he's disappointed in you. Fuck.

"Why are you asking me that, Matt? Why are you questioning me?"

"Why?" he asks. "You're not dumb, Lucas. You're a lot of things, but you're not dumb. You know damn well why I'm asking you that, and now I need you to answer."

I don't know what to say. The question pisses me off and makes me want to scream. That's my first reaction— offense. I know that I missed one practice, and I get why that's important, but is it that serious that my coach needs to question all of my goals and dreams? I'm gonna ask him.

"It was one practice, man. I get that I fucked up. I'm sorry you and Mike were waiting around for me, but. . ."

"Why? Why did you miss? And don't give me that 'I overslept' excuse. I've heard that one enough. I know better. Tell me the truth."

Now I see where he's going with this. I'm dreading

telling him the truth, but I promised him after the last time that I wouldn't lie to him anymore. I'll just have to spill the beans and see how he reacts.

"Alright, I'm gonna level with you, Matt. But I need you to not think that the past is coming back. If I tell you the truth then I need you to trust me that it's not like last time." He doesn't react. No nod, no affirmation of what I'm saying. He just looks at me. "Okay, so here's the truth. I was with a woman. We were together last night, and I really did oversleep. My phone was on vibrate and I didn't hear it. That's the truth. Nothing crazy, nothing like last time."

"There were women last time. Quite a few, if I remember correctly." He's telling the truth. I used to be a fuckboy and a half—a dark period in my life and career where I thought I was King Shit. Matt remembers it well. He remembers it a little too well for comfort.

"Yeah, there were. This is different. I promised you, didn't I?"

"You did."

"And have I done anything to break that trust before today?"

"No, you haven't."

"Right, then can we not Chicken Little this whole situation? The sky isn't falling. I've trained every single day for a month. Never missed a session, never flaked out, never been late to even a single day, have I?"

"No."

"So where is all of this coming from? Are you still treating me like I'm the same guy from a few years ago?"

"It's hard to forget all that."

Ghosts of the past come back to haunt us. The ghosts are our own creations, but that doesn't make them any easier to deal with. A few years ago, I let my ego run out of control. I thought I was better than I was—thought I was more successful than I actually was, and I started surrounding myself with the type of people I should have avoided at all costs. I hung out at clubs late into the night when I should have been resting, I slept around with every random fight groupie who wanted to bang me, and I got into a little trouble with the law. Matt's never forgotten what came of that, and what he had to do to get me back to where I am now.

"I know it is," I tell him. "I get it. But this isn't the past. I'm not fucking around like I was then. I didn't take anything seriously back then and now it's all I think about. I swear, man, you don't have to worry about me like that. My head's in the game."

Matt can be very silent. His silence means different things, depending on what he's thinking or feeling. Usually I can tell if it means he's angry, or disappointed. But I can't tell what he's thinking right now. I keep eye contact with him and wait for him to talk.

"Alright. I'm gonna trust you. But I always remember those times, Lucas. They're not easy to forget. Talk is cheap. You have to show me with your actions that you're as serious as you say you are. No more missed sessions unless it's an emergency, and even then, I want the courtesy of a text or call. And next time you abandon your training partner—who's working with you for free, by the way—he won't stick around for the next camp. Just giving you a warning. There are consequences for things like this."

"That's fair enough. I get it."

Matt extends his hand and I shake it. I can't make any more mistakes or he might not train me for this camp, and I need his Master Splinter mind in order to win my title from

Jason. I have to control things with Mila. I start to walk away when Matt calls out to me.

"Hey." I turn around at the sound of his voice. "Who's the girl? She must be something special for all this."

"Oh," I say. "No one you know."

CHAPTER TWENTY-THREE

LUCAS

The day after I promise Matt I won't miss any more sessions, I meet up with Mila for coffee at a little café in the city. I have practice later, so I wear an old watch that I never wear, just to make sure I can leave in enough time to get to the gym. The last thing I need is more shit. I have a fight coming up, and I need to be focused on my training and my opponent.

My whole mind should be on him. I should be watching footage, putting a picture of him up in the gym so I can look at it when I get tired. All of that should be happening. Don't' get me wrong, I'm focused. Training is going well, my diet is on point, and the early pounds are starting to drop off of me. That's all happening.

But there's Mila also. And she's not just a back-of-my-mind kind of girl. She's renting space in my head, and since we've spent so much time together she's on my mind even more. But now it's more complicated than just a casual thing—now I'm thinking about her so much I've missed practice and gotten into some deep shit with Matt. What am I doing?

I don't have time to think about it. I got to the café ten minutes ago and grabbed a seat outside, and now I see her approaching, looking sexy as ever. "How bad?" she asks. I texted her after the whole thing just to let her know that I had a great time the other night. When she texted me back to ask how everything went with Matt, I was super cryptic, and texted her back 'I'll tell you another time.' I didn't want to talk about it yesterday because I didn't know what to say. Today is 'another time', and I still don't know what to say.

I stand up and hug her. I can't help myself, I take a deep breath of her hair as she leans into me, and as soon as I smell her sweetness I'm right back to that place I was the other night—lost in her. "Not as bad as I thought. Could've been worse. It got a little tense."

"Okay, I have to ask."

"What?"

"I didn't want to say anything when it was happening because you seemed really stressed, but what's the deal with missing a practice? I don't get why it's such a big deal."

"You're a teacher, right?"

"Well, not at the moment, but yeah."

"Imagine if your students had a big test or project that you worked really hard to help them prepare for. You spent hours in the classroom getting them ready, and then you missed a bunch of days of work right before they were going to present it."

"That would be terrible. I would never. . . oh."

"Exactly," I tell her. "Now you get it. Only instead of letting my students down, it's my head coach, my training partners, even my family."

"Oh, I meant to ask you before. You just reminded me.

Speaking of family, how do they feel about your. . . career path? I don't know what to call it."

I smile. "You mean how to do my parents feel about their son throwing knees and elbows at people for a living and barely making ends meet? They're proud as hell, of course." I have to laugh at my own joke, even though it's not a real laugh. It's more of a no-other-emotion-fits-the-moment snicker, and when she senses the sarcasm in my voice she looks at me, waiting for me to finish. "Oh, you want a real answer, huh?"

"Kind of," she says. "But only if you want to talk about it. I was just curious."

This is weird for me. It seems shallow and dumb, but I've never really opened up to a woman before. With the personality that I have, and the amount of time I spend in a gym, I've never had a legit relationship. I've been with a lot of women—especially when I went through my fake celebrity faze a few years back, and I've dated a little, but nothing where a chick was asking about my family or my life outside of the cage.

"It's fine," I tell her. "Ummm. . . I guess saying that 'it's complicated' would be the best way to describe it. Don't get me wrong, I have great parents. Been married forever, grew up in suburbia, went to decent schools, all that. They took me to Matt's gym because I got into a lot of trouble and had some issues in middle and high school. They were desperate and thought the discipline of martial arts would work better than them lecturing me all the time. They were right about that."

"But?"

"How'd you know there'd be a but?"

"Magic," she jokes. "But I know there is one. Tell me."

"But. . . they weren't so thrilled when I took to it so well that I wanted to do it for a living. They didn't like, kick me out of the house or anything, but they weren't calling up my grandparents to brag either. I think they thought that fighting was just going to settle me down until I got to college, and teach me lessons so that I wouldn't get into any more trouble like I had been getting into. I don't think either of my parents even considered that I'd do it full time for money. But they're used to it now."

"And how far can you take this?"

"What do you mean?" I ask, not understanding her question.

She smiles. "If you could push a button right now and have the career path you wanted, what would it look like?"

"Are you interviewing me for a magazine article?" We both laugh.

"Sorry. I'm a teacher, we ask a lot of questions."

"God, I used to hate my teachers. Almost all of them."

"Oh, I'm sorry."

"No, it's okay. That was a while ago. If I had teachers like you I might not have been such a little shit in school."

"Awww. I teach younger grades though, so if I'd had you in class you would have been like eight or so."

"I was a really mature eight-year-old. I still would've thought you were hot. But let me answer you. If I could push a button, I'd be in the UFC. I'd be in a training camp for my first fight in their light heavyweight division, and I'd have my moment—that moment I've always dreamed of."

"Which moment?"

"Where they play my music and call my name in the back. I walk out with my team behind me to adoring fans, cameras in my face, and cheers so deafening that I can't even hear myself think. I see my friends and family in the audience as I make the walk. Then I put in my mouthpiece, hug my team, and step into the octagon as my name is called out for everyone watching on TV to hear. . ."

I trail off. I don't even realize that I've stopped speaking because I get caught up in the imagery in my head. It's a bittersweet thing to picture because it should have happened already. When I come back to reality Mila's looking at me sweetly, not saying a word, just watching me fantasize.

"You'll get there," she says. "You're really good. You have a crazy triangle choke and a great left jab. If you can use those tools, and your defense, you should win against Jason no problem."

It's hard to shock me. I've seen, heard, and even done it all. But I look at Mila like she just turned into an alien right in front of my face. "Wait," I say, smiling. "What the hell? What?" I don't even have words to ask what I want to ask, so I just keep repeating "what?" as she starts to laugh.

"I did a little research," she informs me. "Okay, I did a lot of research."

"On me?" I ask.

"On a little of everything. You. Your fights. At least the ones I could find on YouTube. On fighting stuff, in general. Matt has an online tutorial series."

"Yeah, mostly on Jiu Jitsu techniques, but some striking stuff is on there too. You watched those?"

"I watched like three of them. I started to get confused, but I kind of understood the triangle one."

"Look at you! That's a pretty basic move but it's a little complicated if you don't know Jiu Jitsu. You figured it out?"

"I wouldn't say that I figured it out," she laughs. "But I understand the basic idea. You showed me a closed guard when we had our first lesson. It kind of went from there. I might need a refresher."

"Anytime. It's one of my favorite moves. I've won a few fights by submitting guys who didn't see my set up coming."

"Sometimes it's hard to tell when you're coming. Unless you shout it out of course."

"I like to shout it out."

Here we go again—from fighting to fucking—and now my mind is mush. The best mush possible. If I ever write my autobiography that's a catchy title—'From Fighting to Fucking.' I'm so corny. I smile at the joke in my head.

"I know you do."

We stop for a second and order our coffees from the waitress. It's a beautiful day in early summer. The city is buzzing with human traffic, and the smells of the city are all around us. I love it here. And being with the hottest girl I've ever met isn't a bad way to spend the afternoon. I just have to make sure I get my ass to practice on time.

"So how much trouble did you get in?" she asks. "About missing practice."

"I wouldn't call it trouble. I mean, I'm a grown man and so is Matt, and that was kind of his approach to the whole situation. I know what to do, and I know what not to do. He pretty much told me that if I miss again there are going to be some much more serious consequences."

"Consequences?"

"Like losing my training partners. Some of them fly in or drive pretty far just to do a few rounds with me. Most of them are up-and-coming fighters themselves with the same dreams I have. When I miss, I'm messing up their training too. I get it."

"Is it me?" she asks. "I know you weren't planning this thing between us. Neither of us were. Is it better to lay off while you're training for a fight?"

I wasn't expecting that question. I've asked myself the

same thing, but I always felt guilty about thinking it. I like this girl, a lot, and the more time I'm around her the more that feeling grows. But I also have the opportunity of a lifetime sitting right in front of me, only a few weeks away. I don't know how to answer her. I think about it—maybe a little too long for her comfort, but I want to give it some thought. Finally, I know what the answer is.

"No," I tell her. "Fuck no. Being with someone incredible like you isn't a bad thing. It's me, I'm just not used to it."

"I'm not used to it, either. And also, that might be the sweetest thing anyone's said to me."

"It's true. I just need to be better with my time. If we're together, I have to make sure I don't over sleep or something stupid like that. I can't have anything like that happen leading up to a title fight that could get me that UFC contract."

"We'll make sure. And I love being with you. But that also means not screwing up your dreams. We'll make it work, okay?"

"Deal."

The waitress brings our coffees and I gulp mine down a little fast. "What do you have going on after this?"

"Gonna meet Holly and Sophie. Do some shopping. Maybe some window shopping since I'm on a fixed budget and all."

"Sounds like a plan. I actually have to get going. I have practice."

"Oh, then go for sure. Text me later on."

"I will."

I stand up and hug her. It's everything in my power not to get a full on chubby right there in the café as she presses her body into mine. That would not be a good look at all. I pull back and we kiss.

"Enjoy practice," she says with her cute smile.

I walk away, happier than I've been in a while, and it's a happiness I didn't expect to ever come. I could get used to that.

CHAPTER TWENTY-FOUR

MILA

Lucas turns to leave, and I steal a quick glance at his ass as he walks away. I feel like a guy when I do that, but who cares. I feel better than I have in a long time, except for one thing—I haven't been honest with him. Not completely honest, anyhow. He doesn't know about one of the most important aspects of my recent past, and I feel like I'm lying to him every time I see him. It's bothering me.

I didn't care at first because I was just really attracted to him —there wasn't a whole lot more going on. But the more we hang out and the more we learn about one another, the more I have some real feelings for him, on top of thinking that he's the hottest guy ever.

I have therapy in an hour. I'm going to talk to Dr. Chase about this whole thing and see what he has to say about it. The subway to take me uptown is only a three block walk from the café, but I have to move my ass. He left money for the bill, like the savage gentleman that he is, so I take my last sip before heading to the station.

There are people everywhere, and moving around in Manhattan feels like you're an animal in a herd. I get a little anxious being around all these strangers, especially when they're touching me, but I try to be brave—to remember that I'm the strong person Lucas reminded me I am—that I'm not some victim waiting to be taken advantage of. I'm a strong woman, and this is good practice to remind me of that.

I walk two blocks without any anxiety, and I'm really proud of myself. Even though people are talking and walking all around me, I just keep moving my feet until I'm almost at the station. That's when I hear my phone go off. I reach into my bag and pull it out. The number shows up restricted, but instead of sending it to voicemail I pick up.

"Hello?" I say, stepping to the side of all the traffic. "Who's this?"

What I hear on the other end of the phone sends chills through my entire body. Anxiety doesn't even begin to describe what I feel. When I hang up, I fall to the ground, like a crazy person, and stare off into the distance. The tears come next, and they're uncontrollable.

CHAPTER TWENTY-FIVE

LUCAS

Thank God I got here in time.

Part of me loves training as much as I love fighting.

I've been here for an hour now, and my mind is totally focused. Today is no gi grappling, which is when we do wrestling and Jiu Jitsu, but either bare chested or with rash guards—preferably with rash guards. I got a staph infection once from some dude who was visiting from a gym where they didn't believe in showers—shit almost killed me because I had no idea that I had it until I had to be rushed to the hospital. Now 'no gi' really means 'rash guards.' Luckily Matt is nuts with sanitation and keeping the mats clean.

As I'm rolling with one of the lighter weight guys, John, I start to really get into the groove. You reach a place in training where technique becomes incidental. All the things you learned don't have rehearsed sequences, and your mind doesn't think in terms of steps. At that point you're just in a flow state, and your body moves without your brain requiring any thought to make it do so. I'm not totally there yet, but it's coming along nicely.

I like to practice getting out of bad positions, just in case I get into them on fight night. It's true that my opponent, Jason, never met a performance enhancing drug that he didn't like, but he's also a great fighter without all that crap running through his body. He's medaled in the World Jiu Jitsu Championships a few times, including this past year, in all different weight classes. The kid's no joke on the ground, so my submission game—both offense and defense —needs to be strong.

John and I do a few full rolls with me getting the better of him twice, submitting him with an arm triangle and a knee bar. The third time we went until time was up, but that's mostly because I need to get my cardio up to fight shape. But I'll take it. If I can hang—and even submit a world champion grappler, I have a good chance against Jason.

After our last roll, we shake hands and I grab some water. I don't think I have any sweat left to give. Grappling is the ultimate work out—it works muscles that you didn't know you had. And when you're finished, you feel dead tired and full of energy at the same time. Right now, I'm full of energy, but I need to rehydrate. Matt comes over after the roll.

"You're looking better," he tells me. "Your defense is great, and your killer instinct is coming back. As soon as you saw that arm triangle you dove on it. It was perfect. That's what we need against Jason—if it comes to that."

"What do you mean?"

"Preferably, I'd like to beat him standing. He's not a great striker, and your boxing and Muay Thai is much better than his."

"And my Jiu Jitsu?"

"Is good enough to survive. You might be able to submit

him, but he's never been tapped out before in an MMA fight—only at grappling tournaments, and only by the very best in the world. You remember what GSP says about fighting?"

GSP is the acronym for George 'Rush' St. Pierre—one of the greatest fighters, if not *the* best fighter, to ever live. I used to watch his interviews obsessively, and I've seen his fights so many times that I could practically tell you every move he's ever done in that octagon. He became the best not just because he had amazing skills—which he did—but also because he had one of the best minds in the game. He fought smart. He was never interested in looking tough, or proving anything to anyone. He just wanted to win, and in all of his fights he put himself in positions to win.

"I know," I answer.

"Tell me. I want to hear the words."

"Basically, that you fight where you're strong and your opponent is weak, not the other way around. That gives you the best chance to win."

"Correct. And that strategy served him pretty well, I'd say. If it's good enough for the great GSP, it's good enough for Lucas "The Ghost" Esparza. Yeah?"

"Yeah."

"Pride will get you hurt. We want to win. We want to get into the UFC with a championship belt around our waists."

This is why he's Master Splinter, and why knuckleheads like me need head coaches to do the thinking for us sometimes. Most fighters are hard headed people—we believe that we're the best on the planet, and that no one is stronger or tougher than us. That's why we fight. If we didn't believe that then we'd never get this far to begin with. But the flip side of that coin is that our self belief can become stupidity real quick. I don't want to fight where he's weak and I'm strong—I want to go where he's strongest and prove that I'm even better.

That's my ego.

Those are the moments where I tell humility to fuck off.

That might also be the reason that I'm not a champion right now.

I'm an arrogant prick in the octagon, but I'm also a pretty self-reflective guy when I'm not trying to kill another man for money. The fact of the matter is I didn't just 'get caught' in my last fight. I left my hands down on purpose. I'd been doing that in practice, and none of my sparring partners—Olympic level boxers—could touch me. Sal kept on yelling at me to keep my hands up—that all it takes is one shot one time to get through, and that's it. I didn't listen. I wouldn't listen.

That arrogance cost me everything I'd worked an entire career for up to that point. I'm not going to let that happen again.

"You're right, Splinter."

"I really can't wait for that to go away," he jokes.

"You'll be waiting a while."

Just then I see Matt's face go from a huge smile into a worried look of dread. I turn around to see what he's looking at, and I see Mila running in the door, looking terrified. Matt runs over before I can get there. "What's going on? Mila? Are you okay?"

I don't ask the same question, I wait for her to answer Matt's. She looks panicked, and her eyes are red and puffy like she's been crying. I can see that her mind is all over the place. Her eyes are shooting all over the room and she has little beads of sweat on her forehead.

"Mila, here!" I yell at her only to snap her mind out of

the panic she's obviously feeling. It was the right move, because as soon as I do she looks right into my eyes, and I smile and modulate my tone so as not to panic her. "Tell me what happened."

"Not here," she says. "Not in front of everyone."

I look at Matt and he motions for me to use his office in the back. I pick her up and take her. Everyone is staring again. The poor girl has had two different meltdowns in the gym in a short period of time. But I don't think she cares about other people's perception of her right now. Something is really wrong, and I need to find out what it is.

We get to Matt's office and I shut the door before I lower her to her feet. Guiding her to the couch, I pull her down with me and turn her body to face me.

"Listen to me. Take a couple of big, deep breaths, just like we did at the diner that day. Can you do that with me?" She nods. I model the breathing for her again, and she follows me, in turn. "Good. There we go. Whenever you're ready, I'm here to listen. What is it?"

"I need to tell you something. I'm sorry I didn't tell you before."

"Okay. Whatever it is, it'll be okay."

CHAPTER TWENTY-SIX

MILA

I tell him the story of what just happened. But before that, I tell him *the* story—the story of why I have such bad anxiety. The story of why Holly dragged me to a self-defense class. I tell him everything and hope he isn't angry with me. He just listens, never interrupting, and waits for me to finish before he asks me a few questions.

"This guy you were dating. . ."

"Brett."

"Brett, right. You said he's in prison?"

"Yes. Not for nearly long enough, but he had a great lawyer. He comes from money and they're one of those families that have a lawyer on retainer at all times. He's gotten them out of all sorts of shady business deals and petty crimes through the years."

"Why didn't you tell me all of this?"

There is it—the question I've been hoping he wouldn't ask. I'm not sure I even have a good answer, but he deserves something from me. "This is going to sound weird."

"Try me."

"I didn't want to remember any of that when we were together. You're honestly the first thing in my life since the beating that's made me forget about it. Normally I'd think of it 24/7. At home, with friends, when I'm out. But when we're together, I don't think about anything but you, and I didn't want to mix the two. I honestly wasn't trying to keep it from you, or be deceptive."

"So, I'm guessing the thing about your job was. . ."

"That was a lie and I'm really *really* sorry for that. You didn't deserve to have me lie to you. The truth is I wasn't laid off because of budget cuts—I had to take leave. First it was a medical leave because of my injuries, but after that it was psychological. I couldn't deal with the stress of work. I couldn't even deal with the stress of going to work or being around people. So instead of going to the classroom every day, I went to therapy. I have a great therapist, but it's still a lot of work."

"So, what happened before? The call. You said it was his brother?"

"Wyatt. Real piece of work. CEO of a huge chemical company in Connecticut."

"Of course he is. Go on."

"I haven't seen or spoken to him since the trial when I testified against his brother. And even there, he was shooting me dirty looks and whispering shit under his breath. He's a loose canon—typical corporate type. Entitled, used to getting what he wants. He never liked the idea of me being with Brett to begin with."

"And tell me what he said to you. Exactly."

"At first I didn't know who it was. It was right after you left to come to practice. I was walking to the station to go to therapy and my cell rang. The number was blocked, but for some reason I answered the call. It took me a minute to even realize who it was. That's when he told me he was coming to get me back for what I did to his brother."

"Those were his exact words? 'Coming to get you'?"

"Yeah. I think so. After that I had a panic attack. It was like all the anxiety that'd I'd been fighting off rushed back to the surface all at once. It took over my entire body and I couldn't breathe. It took everything I had for me to even make it to the gym, but you were the first person I thought of seeing. That's why I came here."

"You did the right thing. I'm going to keep you safe."

"How? He knows where I live."

"Well that's the first thing we're going to fix. You're moving in with me."

"I'm what?"

"Hey, look, it doesn't mean we're getting married or anything, but the easiest thing to do is for you to stay at my place. I'll assume he knows where your best friends live so it makes more sense for you to move somewhere he doesn't know, temporarily. I don't know how credible his threat is —I mean, maybe he was drunk and angry and just saying crazy shit. But if he's at all serious, I don't want you staying home alone. You're coming to my place. You can have the bedroom, I'll sleep on the couch if you need me to."

"I think we're past that point, Lucas. We can sleep in the same bed together."

"Yeah, you're right."

I smile. It's the first time I've smiled since I saw him last at the cafe. He's my only reason to smile lately, and even though I'm far from okay, being around him—just being in his presence—is making me feel safe. "I'm so sorry I'm bringing this to your doorstep—literally. I know you have this big fight and the last thing you need on top of that stress is my drama, but. . ."

"Stop it," he says, putting a single, gentle finger over my mouth. I stop talking instantly, and he moves his hand from my mouth to my cheek. "Don't apologize. Yeah, I have a huge fight and all that comes with it. I know it's my dream. And I'm going to get that done, don't you worry. But I also have you—if I have you, that is. I mean, I'm not sure what to call what we are to each other, but. . ."

"You have me," I tell him, tears forming in my eyes. "I don't need a title. I just need you."

"You always have me. And I'm going to keep you safe and help you get through this, okay? Trust me."

"I do trust you. I trust you more than anyone."

"Good. Let me get cleaned up. If it's okay, I want to tell Matt about what's going on. I think he knows some of the backstory."

"He does," I confirm. "Holly told him before I took my lesson with you."

"Okay. Matt will help us move you. He has a huge truck that we can load important stuff into if we need it."

"That sounds great. But won't he be mad about us?"

"Not important. He can be mad, I'll deal with that. But he's also a good guy and he'd want to help you more than he'd want to yell at me. I trust Matt with my life."

"Alright," I tell him. "As long as it's okay. I don't want to get you in trouble again."

"You didn't get me in trouble the first time—that was my own irresponsibility. It had nothing to do with you. Don't worry about me right now. It's okay to be selfish."

"Thank you, Lucas. For everything. I feel better, even though nothing's changed."

"Good," he tells me. "But there is one condition I have."

"Anything. Name it."

"It's time for you to start training—full time."

I love the idea.

I love all that he's doing for me.

And I think that I love him, too.

CHAPTER TWENTY-SEVEN

LUCAS

One month later

It's rare that I feel pride in another person, but I feel it right now.

I've been proud of myself before. When I got my Jiu Jitsu black belt, when I won my first fight, when I first fought for a title. But right now, I'm beaming with pride as I watch Mila lock up a vicious triangle choke on Matt "the Second."

"Don't be a hero, Matt. Tap."

He does what I tell him. After trying to get out and realizing that it's way too tight for an escape, Matt "the Second" taps his hands against Mila's thigh and she relents. The kid's face looks like a bottle of ketchup. He takes a deep breath once he's free and taps hands with Mila.

"Damn, that was tight," he tells her.

"Thanks. I've been working on it."

I had this idea after Mila's trouble with her ex's brother. The scumbag has yet to show himself or make any more threats, but that doesn't mean shit to me. For all I know he's a complete psycho, waiting for his moment. Maybe I'm wrong. Maybe it was just some bitter, drunken threat that he regretted right after he called. I'd like to believe the latter, but I know people too well, and I'm a paranoid fuck when it comes to situations like this.

Mila's been living with me for the past four weeks, and it's honestly been amazing. I was worried. I've never lived with a girl before, and I'm a savage when it comes to my place. There's shit everywhere, and dishes are usually in a giant pile, when I even cook for myself. But she did her thing as soon as she got there—now all my clothes are in a closet, all my dishes get washed right away, and my place looks like I have a full-time maid. She didn't have to do any of that, but I wasn't about to refuse either.

"Okay, one more roll. Two minutes. Matt, you're on your back. You're trying to stand up. Mila, you're trying to keep him down and/or submit. Got it?" They both nod. "Okay, go." I hit my stopwatch for two minutes. They slap hands and start their drill. My idea was to kill two birds with one stone, and so far it's working out beautifully.

I didn't see it at first, but Matt "the Second" and Mila have a lot in common. They've both been victimized by other people—had their confidence and even their dignity taken against their will, and both came to me a broken version of who they really are. Once Mila told me the truth about her past it just clicked that I could help them both. But even more, they could help each other. Four weeks isn't a long time, but for them it's been like a year of training.

"Retain guard, Matt. Don't let her pass!"

"Yes, sir."

First off, I can tell that Matt's got a crush on Mila, and who could blame him? I wish I was rolling around on the ground with a hot girl when I was his age. And she's been really good for him. Not only are they at the same level of training—basically no real level—but she's also helped build his confidence by paying him little compliments here and there. He's done the same. Since he got into that scrap, we started training for real. I taught him all of the basic self-defense moves that he'd need in a real-life situation, and with my assistance he also showed them to Mila. We work once a day on self-defense, we go for a run three times a week, and in between we do real Jiu Jitsu. I was surprised how fast Mila took to grappling. She's tapping Matt left and right, and hanging in there with some of the white belts who have more experience than her.

I also enrolled her in an all female self-defense class we offer at the academy, and she's been learning some specific moves to defend herself in scenarios that women find themselves in, like getting assaulted in a car or in a confined space, or by a much larger opponent. She's doing great, and I can see her confidence building more and more each day. She's like a whole new woman.

"And. . . time! Good job, shake hands. Great job today, Matt."

"Thanks, Professor. It's getting easier."

"That's what I love to hear. Anyone messing with you at school? Tell me the truth."

"One kid tried, but when he saw that I was willing to fight him—even though I didn't really want to—he backed right off. Other than that, there hasn't been any trouble."

"Good," I tell him, putting my hand on his shoulder. "Let's keep it that way."

"Yes, Professor."

Matt's dad takes him home right after the roll and Mila stays behind to watch me train. I've been so caught up in teaching and taking care of Mila that I sometimes forget that my championship fight is coming up in about a month. So far there's been no bullshit. I've been in the gym and on the mats every single day, even with a teaching schedule that Master Splinter luckily pulled back to just Matt "the Second." Other than that, I feel good. I can't wait to get my hands on Jason, and to get that gold strap wrapped around my waist once and for all.

Mike is back for a training session. Matt's convinced that my best shot for beating Jason is on my feet, and I agree. Jason's an okay striker, but he's a great grappler. It's a better idea to use my punches and kicks to keep the fight standing than it is to go on some ego trip on the ground. That means that I need my hands sharp, and Mike is just the guy to help me with that.

The guy's always on time. He walks into the gym, shades on, attitude radiating off of him. It's not a bad attitude, it's just that type all of us fighters have when it's time for business. Outside of the cage most fighters you meet are nice, humble, genuinely nice people. But when it's time to make the donuts, watch out. Then we all think we're king of the fucking world.

"You ready, bitch?" he says in his thick Brighton Beach Russian accent. "I'm gonna make that face ugly."

Mila looks at me. "Who's that? And does he always talk to you like that?"

"That's Mikhail—we call him Mike cause we're dumb Americans— and yeah, that's his thing. He likes to shit talk all of his training partners and try to get into their heads. It's a good exercise. It's hilarious when he does it in fights—you should see the looks on his opponent's face when he starts talking shit about their moms."

"Oh, okay. Got it," she says awkwardly. "There's a lot about fighting culture I guess I still don't get."

"Ha," I laugh. "That was mild. You have no idea."

Mila stays as Mike and I go five rounds. We're not going full tilt like they used to in the old days. Old school gym guys used to fight their teammates and call it sparring, but what it really did was lead to a shorter career and more brain damage. However many blows to the head a guy would take over the course of a career in the cage or octagon, he'd take tens of thousands more in the gym training for those fights. Nowadays, because of the knowledge about CTE and brain trauma, a lot of top guys don't even spar any more. I go light, just drilling technique, but neither Mike nor I are hitting each other full force. It's mostly for timing and developing reaction time.

In between rounds, I catch glimpses of Mila watching me—sweaty, shirt off, breathing heavy—and I feel like showing off. I resist the urge because training camp isn't the place to get yourself hurt or hurt your partner, but whenever she's around I want to showboat—to puff out my chest and dance around that cage like Muhammad Ali, cocky and confident all at the same time. She brings that out in me—something carnal that makes me want to show her that I'm king of this fucking jungle.

When our session is over, Mila decides to take off to meet up with her friends. I still have a strength and conditioning session, and Matt and I want to do some game planning. And it's that part—the thinking part, where Matt really earns his Master Splinter status. He's a legit genius when it comes to fight strategies. He watches hours upon hours of footage on guys—studies their tendencies, their strengths, their weaknesses—and then he puts together a game plan for his guys for fight day based on all that research. I can't wait to hear what he has to say, but first I need to get that cardio in.

"How about Chinese later? I haven't had Chinese in a few weeks."

This is another one of those moments where Mila doesn't fully get the fight game. A huge part of this fighting profession isn't fighting at all—its weight cutting. Almost no pro fighter actually walks around at the weight he or she fights at. We all walk around much heavier, and we cut down so that we'll have a size advantage over our opponents. I'm not doing the week-of-the-fight weight cut just yet, but I am cutting weight, which basically means no food that tastes good.

"Weight," is all I say.

"Shit, I keep forgetting, I'm sorry. I see you eating all of those prepared meals, I should probably remember, right?"

"Nah, it takes some getting used to. Normal people don't try to lose thirty pounds in a month. Just us crazy folk. But you don't have to suffer. You want me to pick up Chinese to bring home later?"

"Are you sure?"

"Yeah, it's fine, I don't mind. Just text me what you want and I'll grab it. What time are you home?"

"Seven. I'm meeting Holly and Sophie for a drink but they have to leave by 6:30, so should be home by seven."

"Perfect," I say.

"I'll see you then. Thank you!"

We kiss before she leaves, and I do it right in front of Matt on purpose. I'm not trying to rub it in his face or anything like that, but he was not so thrilled when I told him about us. Like I said, we're two grown men, and he's not going to lecture me, but I know him well enough to know when he's not happy with something. So instead of arguing with him, I just need to show him that being with a woman and training aren't incompatible things with me—I can handle both and do well.

"I love those lips."

"I love yours even more. Text me your order later."

"I will. Enjoy cardio."

"If you ever did this kind of cardio you wouldn't say that to me."

She smiles and walks off.

I have cardio. I have game planning. I have a fight. But all I really want is for the next few hours to pass so that I can be with her again.

CHAPTER TWENTY-EIGHT

MILA

"My whole body hurts, you guys."

"Ohh," Sophie says, a little too enthusiastically. "He's athletic in and out of the cage, huh? I need details. Does he like, throw you around the bedroom?"

The image isn't completely unpleasant, but I have to smile at Sophie's particular kind of sexual imagination. "Of course he does. Picks me up, throws me around, catches me like I'm a ball. It's insane. We should be in porn, we'd make a fortune. Next time I'll invite you over to watch."

"Really?"

I don't know which scenario is scarier—if she's joking, or if she's not joking.

"No, not really. Jesus, Sophie."

"Oh, yeah. I was just playing around anyhow. I knew you were joking."

"Yeah, sure," Holly says, finally interjecting into this ridiculous conversation. "He's been working you hard, huh? At the gym, I mean."

"I've never worked so hard at something in my life. It's

so difficult and so much fun all at the same time. And having Lucas as a teacher doesn't hurt either."

"I bet it doesn't. And to think, you have me to thank for it all!"

"Woah, woah, woah. How do you figure?"

"Are you kidding?" she asks. "You didn't want to go to the gym. I forced you. If I hadn't, you would have never met Lucas, and you never would have ended up together. It's simple."

"So, by that logic, I should thank Matt also, because he arranged for Lucas to be my teacher. And I should thank the girl who canceled also. I guess I have everyone to thank for us getting together."

"Now you're starting to understand," she laughs. "But seriously, I'm so happy for you. We both are."

"I'm not so sure if Sophie's happy, or just wants to hear about the sex."

"I'm gonna be honest, it's a little of both. But look, you were the one who was screaming out about his huge dick in pubic, so don't make me out to be the freak of the group."

"Who are you kidding, Sophie, you are the freak of the group." Holly turns to her and raises an eyebrow. "Our girl here is just appreciating a well-endowed man. It'd been a while for her and she got excited. You, on the other hand, would be asking if they'd tried anal yet. Big difference."

Sophie just sits there and so do I. I've never been one to talk openly about my sex life, even with my closest friends. But like everything else with Lucas, I'm different than my normal self. I'm Mila 2.0, and I'm loving this new me—the one who talks about the size of her man's dick to her friends. Sophie and I look at each other, and I brace myself for the question I know is coming.

"Well. . ." she asks. "Have you?"

We all start cracking up. Once again, I get the crazy looks from everyone around us for talking about dicks with my girlfriends. Eh, so what?

<><><>

Sophie and Holly head off where they're going next. They invited me to go with them, but I've become *that* friend—the bad one who'd rather hang out with her boyfriend than her friends. It's not really an either/or thing for me, but I really feel better when I'm around him. I feel secure, I feel confident, and that's really what I need right now with everything that's been going on. On top of that, I think I've been good for him too. I like supporting him, cheering him on, helping him to realize the dreams he's always had. We're not just hot for one another—we're good for one another.

And how many guys would just hand over a spare key to their apartment just like that after dating a girl for just a few weeks? Not many, but Lucas isn't like most guys. Not how he looks, not in what he does, and not in how he behaves with me. I texted him my order while walking back to his place, and I'm secretly—okay, not so secretly—excited about Chinese take out. I went a little later with the girls than I thought. It's almost seven now, so I head up to set the table for when Lucas gets back.

As I put the key in the door I hear footsteps from behind me. I don't turn around like I normally would because I'm practicing my confidence. But when I hear those same footsteps approaching me I turn my head. I don't even realize that I've screamed, but I did. I turn around, struggling to turn the key in the lock faster. I hear a click as the footsteps get even closer, moving faster. I push the door open with all of my strength, and just as I'm about to step through the doorway I feel my entire body being pushed through space, and by the time I realize what's happened I'm on the ground.

I look up and see Wyatt standing over me. He's wearing a black overcoat and sunglasses—like a bad disguise in an old spy movie. He takes his glasses off right away, and all of who he is comes flooding back to me. It's one thing seeing someone a long time ago, or hearing their voice on the end of a bad cell phone connection—it's another thing to see them again in person. It brings everything back, and for a second, I really think he's going to pull out a gun and kill me.

Jesus, how did he find me?

CHAPTER TWENTY-NINE

LUCAS

That girl really loves her Chinese take out.

This is the third time she's asked in two weeks to get it. Each time I tell her I'm cutting weight, which she usually remembers, but she's got a one-track mind when it comes to chicken lo mein and pork fried dumplings. It's not fair—that shit smells so good that for a second—and only a second—I think about opening up that container and cheating on my diet. The last thing I need is Matt and Mila mad at me for eating two stupid dumplings. Three—I'd definitely eat three.

I use all the self control that I have to just pay the guy and take the bag. It's a short walk to my place so the food will still be hot when I get there. I'm dog tired from that cardio session today—I've never gone so hard in my life, but it'll pay dividends when I'm deep into the third round.

But I've dedicated enough of myself to the fight game today—physically and mentally—now it's time to wind down and enjoy some good food. . . scratch that, watch her enjoy some good food, while enjoying her company. Some

R & R would do me good right now. I do one last cardio session by charging up the stairs to the third floor where my place is, pushing as hard as I can while balancing a brown bag of take out. It's a feat to be witnessed, only I'm all alone. But not for long. . .

I hear something inside. First, I think it's my imagination—that Mila has the TV blasting, but she doesn't really do that. I step up to the door and get my keys out of my pocket. It's not the TV—there's something going on in there. As I struggle to turn the key I hear the sounds of things crashing, and I hear Mila calling out.

Fuck the keys.

I take a giant step back and run, full force, into the door, shoulder first, the bag of take out a forgotten mess on the hallway floor. It flies open as I burst through the doorway. My eyes scan the room and I see a man on top of Mila. At first, I panic because I think he's hurting her, but as I rush over I see that she has him in her full guard—her legs wrapped around his waist, ankles locked, and she's controlling his posture by wrapping one arm around his neck and hooking his other arm with her arm.

Good girl. Jiu-Jitsu self defense 101—whoever controls the distance controls the damage. As long as she holds him to her body he can't hurt her, but it's all strength. She doesn't have long before her arms will crap out. I sprint the rest of the way to them, faster than I've run in my life, and grab him by the arm. Most people think the best way to pull someone off someone else is to grab their body and pull, but the best way is to drag their arm. I grip one of his wrists with both of my hands and then circle behind him.

"Let go of him!" I yell.

She opens her guard immediately and I pull him off. My adrenaline's pumping, but not nearly as much as his is about to be. I let go of his wrist and he falls on the ground, onto his back. I follow him down, right into full mount. It's incredible what training does for you—even in this crazy situation my body just responds. It's just muscle memory. I didn't ask who he was, what he was doing, or what was going on—I just become the grappler I'm trained to be, and this mothafucker is about to be in a world of hurt.

They called the great Mark Coleman the "Godfather of Ground-and-Pound", but that's only because 'they' never saw me right now. With this man trapped underneath me, I lay into him with all the fury I have inside of me. I drop elbows like rain, and when I feel a few of them get through, he starts to turtle up. That's when I start to drop fists on him.

One after the other. Brutal punches. One at a time, until I lose count. I feel his nose break when I get a clean shot with my right hand, and once he stops fighting I know it's over. I jump off of him as fast as I jumped on him. And once I'm sure he'd down and knocked out, I run to Mila, who's still on her back, crying hysterically.

"It's okay. He's not going to hurt you. Are you okay?"

"I. . . think. . . so."

She's sobbing, and I hold her close to my body for comfort. "It's okay. You're okay. I got him. He's down." I look over at his limp body, getting my first real look at him and realize who he is. The first thought I have is hoping that he's alive. The man needs to stand trial like his piece of shit brother. I can't believe he came here. How did he ever find this place? "I need to call the police right now. Can you sit here while I call? I'm going to be right here, don't worry."

"Uh-huh."

"Good. Sit tight."

I reach into my pocket to pull out my phone, and as

soon as I do I know that something's wrong. I drop the phone on the floor, and Mila looks up at me with teary eyes.

"What's the matter, Lucas?"

I take a deep breath before I say the words I'm about to say. "I think. . . I think I may have broken my hand."

CHAPTER THIRTY

LUCAS

The Next Day

My fight—the only fight that's ever mattered—is in three weeks, and I'm sitting here waiting to hear if I can even make it to the cage. Matt's waiting for a text to find out if we need to pull out, and Mila is sitting in the waiting room.

That piece of shit who broke into my house got the worst of it. My hand might be fucked up, but his face is going to need reconstructive surgery. I laid into him good—better than I should have. I wasn't thinking about my own well being, or keeping my body intact for the fight. I wasn't thinking at all, I just reacted like I've been trained to do. I should have dropped more elbows or used my Jiu Jitsu to choke him out or break his arm, but my brain wasn't doing much critical thinking in the heat of the moment.

The cops came, arrested Wyatt, took statements from me and Mila, and that was that. It was a pretty open and shut kind of situation. Between the call to Mila's cell, the pushed in door, the state of my place, and a bunch of other evidence that clearly showed he stalked Mila and broke into my place to attack her, Wyatt was in deep shit. I'm probably going to have to testify against him at some point, but he's going away one way or the other. Good. Sometimes the bad guys get what they deserve. I just hope this didn't send Mila back to having bad anxiety again. She was doing so good.

The doctor walks in holding up an x-ray. I can read his energy before he opens up his mouth to tell me the bad news. I brace myself.

"Mr. Esparza, how are you feeling?"

"I've been better, doc. You?"

"I'm good, thanks. Look I know this is very consequential to you, so I'm not going to beat around the bush. Your hand is severely fractured."

Fuck! Fuck! Fuck!

Part of me already suspected that. Part of me knew deep down. The rest of me was in total denial. Now I have to face the truth of that x-ray. Matt's gonna flip the fuck out.

"I see. Does that mean I can't fight?"

"When is your fight?"

"A few weeks."

"It would be medically inadvisable to strike anything with your hand for several months, and really not at all. That's how this happened in the first place."

No, doc. This happened because I was brutally beating someone who tried to assault my girlfriend—but you don't need to know about that.

"Right," I say, lost in my own thoughts. "So, theoretically, if I did hit something with this hand?"

"You would fracture it in even more places, and there's a chance you'd never fully heal correctly. To state it plainly, son, it could end your career if you try to use it before it fully heals."

It's rare in life that you get to hear the exact

combination of words that you never want to hear strung together. This is one of those moments for me. I really can't believe that this is happening right now. Of all the shit timing. I try not to freak out. The doctor doesn't deserve the shit show of what it would look like, so I just thank him and head out.

Mila's waiting for me, and when she seems me coming out of the back she stands up and we make eye contact. I know what my face looks like right now, and it isn't pleasant. She can read that it's bad news, and after signing out we walk out of the doctor's office in silence.

When we're in the parking lot is when she finally breaks the silence.

"How bad?"

"Basically broken. Doctor said if I punch anything with this hand, I could end my career."

"Oh my God, Lucas, I'm so sorry. I can't believe this is happening to you. Your dreams about the UFC—the title fight—all of it. Do you want me to come with you when you tell Matt you're pulling out?"

"No," I tell her. "Because that's not what I'm going to tell Matt. I'm still going to fight."

CHAPTER THIRTY-ONE

LUCAS

I let Mila come with me, but I asked her to stay in the car.

I went in to talk to Matt about everything. The poor guy didn't even know that the break in happened, let alone what came from it. When it's over, I meet her back in the car, and we drive back to the apartment to talk.

The tension in the car is strong. I'm stewing in my anger and frustration while Mila watches me, concern etched all over her face.

"How'd he take the news?" she asks me once we're in my apartment.

"Which news? The break in? Or the legal issues? Or my broken hand?"

"Any of it," she says. "All of it. Whatever you want to talk about."

I feel anger rising from the pit of my stomach. It's intense and sudden, and it feels like the type of thing that's going to boil over if I'm not careful. I should say nothing—I should fake a headache and go lie down and hope that when

I wake up I'm not as pissed as I am right now. But of course, I don't do that. I open my mouth and start talking.

"Well, let's see. He felt terrible about the break in, which I expected. He was concerned about how you're doing after what happened. Then I told him about my hand and he flipped out like I knew he would. Matt's a pretty level-headed guy, so him going from zero to sixty like that is rare. Then I told him that I wanted to fight despite my broken hand, and he looked at me like I was the biggest asshole in the world."

"Jesus, I'm so sorry."

"Wait," I say, getting pissed again thinking about what just happened. "It gets better, I haven't even gotten to the punch line just yet."

"Oh no."

"He said that if I try to fight anyway, that he's not going to train me or corner me in the fight. That he's not going to be a part of me. . . how did he put it. . . 'Throwing away all of the work everyone's put into me over the years.' Yeah, that was it. I might be off by a word or two but hey, it's hard to remember exact phrases when you're being yelled at and threatened."

I can hear the edge in my voice, it's cutting through the air like a sharpened blade. I really can't help it. There's too much to process right now, and none of it is good. And the more I talk the more I start to feel something else that I didn't expect at all, something I feel guilty about as soon as I realize what it is—I feel resentment towards Mila.

"Lucas, I. . ."

"What? Are you going to say you're sorry again? I don't need an apology. It is what it is."

"You sound mad."

"You think?" I yell. "Why would I be mad? I mean,

what could I possibly have to be angry about? My lifelong trainer telling me he's about to drop me? My fucking hand being broken? The fight that may have gotten me into the UFC being in jeopardy? Not sure why I'd be in such a bad mood."

"I get it. I'm sorry."

"Please stop saying that. Your sorries aren't going to fix my hand. It's broken because of. . ."

I stop short of saying what I really want to say, but I've said too much for it to go unnoticed.

"Because of me," she finishes. "Is that what you were going to say? Your hand is broken because of me?"

"No," I say, calming down just enough to not get crazy. "It's not because of you. It's because of the drama that followed you to my doorstep. I beat Wyatt senseless and I'd do it again in a heartbeat. He was going to hurt you, and he needed to be stopped. But nonetheless, this is what I get. You get saved, he gets thrown in jail, and I get my dreams taken away from me."

"Look, maybe I should go."

"Yeah," I say, my blood still boiling. "Maybe you should."

"Fine. I'll let you lick your wounds."

She sounds hurt as she storms off. Of course she's hurt, I just said some pretty nasty stuff. And the worst part is that I don't totally mean it. What I said is true, but she didn't need to hear it said to her in that way. She doesn't go right to the door and walk out like in a movie—she goes into the bedroom. I hear her scrambling around so I go in there.

"What are you doing?" I ask.

"What does it look like? I'm getting my stuff and leaving. My place is safe now, right? That's why I was staying here in the first place. Wyatt's in jail, so there's no need for me to be here anymore. You seem like you need your space to heal up. It's all good."

Which is code for, 'it's not good at all'—it's the opposite of good.

I don't try to stop her. I don't have the energy. I walk into the living room like a zombie and collapse on my couch. It takes ten minutes for her to get all of her stuff together in the same suitcase she brought it over in. She's moving fast, and I don't blame her. I'm toxic right now, and I just took a world's worth of stuff out on her.

She doesn't even say goodbye, just slams the door behind her, and I'm left alone sitting on my couch, wondering how shit went so far south so quickly.

CHAPTER THIRTY-TWO

MILA

"You haven't spoken to him in two weeks? Mila! You were all hot and heavy, what happened?"

Holly looks genuinely concerned for me—for us, if there is an us to be concerned about. I'm not sure. My experience is that if you pack your stuff, walk out, and don't talk to the other person on the scale of weeks, then you're kind of de facto broken up, but I don't actually know.

"He lost his shit. His hand is fractured, but he was trying to fight anyhow. It went south with his trainer. Came home all angry. Blew up. I walked out 'cause I'm not dealing with any more unstable men in my life."

Holly shoots me a look like she's not buying my liberated woman act—she sees through me sometimes. "Is he unstable? Or were things just falling apart for him in that moment? Because there's a difference, and it's an important one."

"Aren't you supposed to be my friend, Holly? Not his."

"I am your friend. I'm your best friend—which is why I don't want you to throw away the best thing that's come into your life in a long time over a stupid fight. Fights happen. Outbursts happen, but Jesus, Mila, look at what you came from. Lucas didn't hit you, or pound the wall, or threaten you, or say anything so terrible to you. You were head over heels, and then you walked away the second there was conflict. I mean, the man jeopardized his career to save your life."

Hearing the whole thing recounted to me like that makes me feel silly. Maybe there's something to what she's saying.

"Did I fuck this whole thing up?"

"Not exactly," Holly tells me. "You just started dating a fighter. They're a special breed of human being, Mila. How many men do you know, when push comes to shove, who would voluntarily fight other men in a cage?"

"I know a few guys who'd say that they would, but zero who actually would."

"Exactly. No one except Lucas. You're dating yourself a savage, Mila. A little outburst from time to time might come with the territory. Yeah, he lost his cool but was it really that bad, given what happened? He loves you, and he'd do anything to keep you safe. He proved it. Forgive him for the rest."

"Why do you think he loves me?"

"Because he almost killed another man who was trying to hurt you. Because he's been training you to be able to defend yourself when he had the most important fight of his career coming up. Because of the way he looks at you. Trust me, he loves you."

I don't know why—it seems stupid to even admit this to myself—but I've never thought of it that way. He's been so loving to me that I didn't even realize it was loving. Or maybe I'm still so fucked up from how Brett was with me that I wasn't even capable of recognizing real love when it came along. I guess I still have some growth left to make.

"Shit," I say. "I fucked it up. I can't believe this."

I fall down on the couch, tears forming in my eyes. Holly sits next to me and does what she's always done—makes me feel better.

"I doubt it. Someone who loves you like Lucas loves you doesn't just walk away like nothing happened. He's probably thinking that you don't want to be with him because you stormed out and haven't spoken to him since. You think if you called or texted that he wouldn't respond?"

"He'd respond."

"So? What are you waiting for?"

"I don't know. It might be a little awkward at this point, don't you think?"

"Yeah, maybe," she says. "But I'd take awkward over sad and lonely any day of the week."

The woman has a point. She always has good points. "Maybe I'll reach out."

"I think that you should. But, even if you chicken out, here." She reaches into her bag and pulls out an envelope. The front of it reads *A Girls Night Out*. "From Sophie and I. A little gift for all the progress you've made."

"What is it?"

"Open it up."

Inside there's a piece of paper and three tickets. The paper reads 'I can't believe we're going to a stupid fight, but we'd do anything to make sure you're happy. Love, Your Girls.' Inside is three front row tickets to Lucas' fight on Saturday night. I look up at her confused.

"We're going to the fight together?"

"Your powers of perception are amazing. Yes, girl, we're going to see hot half naked men beat each other up."

My confusion turns to happiness. I normally hate surprises, but this is the best one I can remember. My girls are there for me even when I'm too stubborn to be there for myself. I'll still reach out to Lucas, but if he can't get back to me, I'll be there for him, win, lose, or draw—hopefully win.

"I love you guys."

"We love you too," she says.

CHAPTER THIRTY-THREE

LUCAS

Fight Week

It's Thursday.

The fight is on Saturday and I'm by myself. Well, I'm almost by myself.

"Hey you broken-handed motherfucker!"

"Shut the fuck up, someone will hear you."

Damien. That's Damien.

"I don't give a fuuuuuckk," he yells, smiling like a jack ass the entire time.

I grab him. It's not hard, he's smaller than me, but not by a whole lot. Damien's another fighter at my gym. Scratch that—Damien is *the* fighter at my gym. He's the best of all of us, and that's saying something because we have a nice stable of up and coming guys. He fights welterweight—170 pounds, and he's a fucking killer. He's been away for the past year training Muay Thai in Thailand because, well, that's the kind of savage that he is. He's young—twenty-two —and a wild motherfucker if ever there was one. But he's also a great dude who's willing to help me out when no one else will. On top of that, he also lost his last fight, something that still eats at him like crazy.

"I give a fuck, so stop. Seriously, I'm already on my own with this, I don't need to piss anyone else here off."

"I'm hurt. How can you be alone when I'm here?" He makes a fake crying face then starts laughing. I can't help but smile. He's serious as a heart attack when it comes to training and his career, but outside of that he's a goofball.

"Fine," I concede. "I'm not alone. I have the great Damien with me."

"That's right, fuck-face, and we're gonna smoke this fool, gimp hand or no gimp hand."

"You have such a delicate way of saying things."

"One of my many, many. . . oh, did I mention *many* talents!"

"As long as you stay humble about it," I joke.

"Eh, humility is for pussies. I'll save my humility for when I'm learning things—that's really the only time it's needed. But outside of that. . ." He points to his shirt—a jet black tee with the words "Fuck The World" in giant white capital letters. Damien is many things, but subtle he is not.

"You sure it's okay to use the facilities?" I ask. "Matt. . ."

"I talked to Matt, it's fine. We just have to use it at odd hours when no one else is around. You know how he is."

Yeah, I know how he is. He's stubborn, old school, and even though I understand his decision, it's still eating at me that he'll let me go into the most important fight of my life without him or his coaching staff.

"This is a dick move on his part, I'm sorry."

"Don't apologize," Damien says. "It is a dick move. But so was how you acted more than once. So is how I've acted a few times in the past. That's the thing about being a dick, brother, we all do it on a semi-regular basis. In this particular case, he's not going into a fight with an injured fighter. You want him to lose his credibility as a trainer?"

That was a sticking point with Matt. Yes, he was pissed that I broke my hand, but he understood that I had nothing to do with causing that situation. The real issue between us was about the fight—he offered to cancel the fight, let me heal up, then resume training and—hopefully—get a rematch when I was better. But that whole process could have been a year, at least, and there was no guarantee that Jason would even be around. Or my replacement opponent could have gone in there, smoked Jason in ten second, and gotten a sweet UFC contract that should have been mine. I wasn't willing to wait, even though it would have been the smart thing to do.

I was willing to risk it all—my health, my career, my everything—in order for a chance to beat a guy I know I can beat, even with one hand. Matt was not. He wasn't comfortable training me with the risk of fucking up my hand, or having one of the other guys feel guilty about accidentally injuring me. Matt's not a risk taker like that—he has a business to run that's bigger than just me, and even though I get it, like I said, I'm not a gym owner. I'm a fighter, and if I have to do this alone, then that's what I'm gonna do. It just sucks Matt won't be there. I could really use him.

"No, I get his point of view, I just. . ."

"What? Wanted him to be a crazy bastard like you? Want him to risk feeding his family and the business his father started, all because you don't want to rehab your hand? Come on now! You're not selfish like that."

Fuck you for being so reasonable, Damien. I expect better of you.

"So, I fucked up with not one, but two different people in my life I care for. Great."

"Oh yeah," Damien says. "That chick. What's her name?"

"Mila."

"Mila, right. You texted me that picture of her—she's smoking hot."

"I know. And speaking of which, it took you forever to get back to me."

"Thailand, dude. How strong of a WiFi signal do you think they have in the jungles of Southeast Asia?"

"Fair enough."

"I'll run point for you on Matt's end—he loves me. I can talk to him about anything. I'll see what I can do. But the girl? That's all you, bro?"

It sure is all me. I've got to do something about that whole situation. I don't think I said anything too crazy, but then again, I'm dealing with a woman who was almost beaten to death by her ex and then assaulted by the guy's brother. I've got to make that whole thing right again.

"I'll deal with that," I tell him. "But right now, we need to game plan. You and me."

"Let's do it, bro. You know I always have ideas."

Before I get to hear his ideas, I hear a sound from my bag. I thought that I turned my phone off, but I guess I forgot. I run over as Damien rolls his eyes at me. "Relax," I tell him. My phone never makes me smile, but right now it does. It's a text from Mila.

Mila: Hey. We need to talk. I'm not angry. After your fight or whenever, text me. I'll wait.

I smile but then put my phone right away. I have to compartmentalize right now. I can't get caught up in any relationship drama until after Jason and I have had our date in the octagon.

"Let's go, man!"

"Shut the fuck up, I'm coming. Shit, you'd think it was you who had the fight of his life coming up."

"I'm in there with you, brother, so it may as well be me."

Damien's like a brother, but what he's never experienced—to my knowledge—is a woman like Mila. If he had, he'd also take a few seconds before his last day of training to stare at his phone and smile, just like I'm doing right now.

<><><>

It's Friday night.

Weigh-ins.

Cutting weight is the worst part of fighting. Worse than getting punched. Worse than leg kicks. Worse than getting choked unconscious. Your body is literally eating itself. Some guys look like the men in scenes from World War II movies when a concentration camp is liberated. What cutting weight means is that we're shedding water weight—basically dehydrating ourselves—so that the pounds drop off of us quicker than normal.

Fighters have to weigh in at our contracted weight. For Jason and I, that weight is two hundred and five pounds. One pound over for either of us and the title fight is off, and it just becomes a regular bout. I've done my part, and I hope he's done the same.

The arena that hosts the fights also hosts the Friday weigh ins. All the fighters are miserable—myself include. We're cranky because we're starving, and all I can think about is getting off the scale so that I can eat and drink something.

It's the first time I'm seeing Jason in person since we fought the first time. I have no doubt that scumbag has EPO or some kind of steroid inside of him, but the testing at these lower level shows just isn't there yet. Guys get away with stuff all the time, and some gyms—like Jason's—have a reputation for having dirty fighters.

I see him there, looking as skeletal as me, and his suffering makes me feel better about my own. Even fighters who hate each other have a mutual respect for the weight cut. That's about all I respect of Jason. After we each hit our target weight, we have the face off.

We turn to each other and hit a fight pose. This part I love. Looking into another man's eyes tells you everything that you need to know about him as a fighter. Some guys talk a good game. Some even fake a good game. Trash talk, bravado, posturing, all of it. But the eyes don't lie. The eyes always tell the truth.

And as I look into his, I see that he's ready to lose to me. He wants to. He's ready to surrender that title to me so that I can rise to the top of this game, and he can fall by the wayside, into obscurity.

The stare down ends, and we each turn and go our own ways. Now all the bullshit is over. No more talking, or interviews, or stare downs. Now we fight.

Now, it's time to let us be the savages we are.

CHAPTER THIRTY-FOUR

LUCAS

It's Saturday.

Fight night.

I'm at the hotel with Damien playing video games and drinking water. You take the little things in life for granted until they're denied to you. Even simple things like a sandwich and water can taste like the best thing you've ever consumed when you've been cutting weight for days prior. Now my weight is back up to normal. Right now, I'm two hundred and twenty-five pounds. The commissions only care that you weigh in at your agreed upon weight the night before—in the twenty-four hours after that, you can balloon up as large as you'd like—and most guys do. It isn't uncommon for guys to fight ten, twenty, even thirty pounds *above* their listed weight class come fight night. For me the number is twenty, and I feel like my old self once I have some calories and water in me.

"Jump, asshole, jump!"

Damien gets into his video games. He's like a big kid—a big, violent kid who's one of the best strikers in the world.

His silliness distracts me from all the doubt going through my head. Most guys won't admit to those kind of thoughts—they want to put up a front like they're world beaters—they're not afraid of anything or anyone, but that's all bullshit. We're all afraid—not of our opponents, or of getting hurt like regular people—we're scared of failure, of losing, of being embarrassed in front of a room full of people, of letting our teams down after months of work.

But I'm trying to block the fear out. There's nothing it's going to do but get me hurt. I look at my phone, which I never do this close to leaving for the arena, and I see one more text from Mila, wishing me good luck. It's the boost of confidence I really need.

No matter what happens out there—if I win or if I don't—I need to try and make things right with her. I was falling in love with her, big time, and for a guy like me to admit something like that takes a lot. Fighters are selfish—we live for our own dreams and aspirations—but I've spent the last few months thinking about her, worrying about her issues, and trying to keep her safe, sometimes at the cost of my own dreams. That means something. It's not a mistake, or me not caring about all that I want to do, it tells me that she's the one—the girl I'm meant to be with. I have to make it work. I text her back real quick so she doesn't think I'm ignoring her, then my phone goes off. She knows it's fight night, and now my focus has to shift to where it belongs—towards ending the night of Jason.

I'm shit at video games right now because I basically have one hand. It's getting better, but even when I bump against something or try to grab the handle on my bag it hurts. I try to play with Damien but he notices right away.

"Yo, let's stop. Put the controller down, I'll play one

player vs. the computer. You can watch me whoop ass, then I'll do the same for you later on."

"Yeah," I concede, putting my controller down. "I don't need to go out on a video game related injury. I'd be the laughing stock of the internet."

"Bitch, you think anyone knows who you are yet?"

I laugh. "After tonight they will. They'll all know me then. I promise you that."

Damien's silliness taps into the intensity that lies just underneath. He looks at me with fixed eyes and a twisted smile. "That's fucking right. We win with one hand or with two. This is meant to be."

"That's right. Now let's go to the arena."

I'm warming up in the back. It's almost my turn to fight.

Local shows are a different animal than big events like the UFC puts on. There are fewer people, it's less professional, and there are fewer fights. I know Matt's in the building because one the female fighters at our gym was also early on the card, but she's in a different locker room. I haven't seen Matt at all in weeks, and I'm not about to chase him down now. He did what he felt he had to do, and so did I. Besides, I have Damien, and I'm about a half hour away from punching Jason in the face—with my left hand, anyway.

The last bout before mine is getting started—I hear the names of the other guys being called out, and the sounds of that, coupled with the roar of the crowd, kicks my body into fight mode. The rational part of my brain starts to shut down, and I have a focus unlike any other.

Damien stepped out to get some water, and I'm shadow

boxing in the corner. Half of this is a show—I don't want any of the other fighters to have any indication that I'm hurt. I throw my right like there's nothing wrong with it, even though I know I'd break it badly if it were a person and not the air I was throwing at. No one goes into a fight healthy. It's just a matter of how hurt you are, and how well you can mask it from your opponent. I'm doing my best, but in the back of my mind I'm still worried.

I throw some combinations to get a sweat going, then practice a few double legs. I just want my muscles to be warm enough so that I'm loose out there. I keep throwing the same combination—jab, jab, cross, then shoot in for a takedown—over and over. It's the one Damien and I have been practicing so that I can grapple with Jason rather than strike with him. I do it about three times in a row, when I hear a voice from behind me.

"You're dropping your left when you throw that cross." I'd recognize Master Splinter's voice anywhere. I turn around and see him standing there with Damien, who's grinning like a kid on Christmas.

"He's right. We worked on that, bro."

"Damien, give us a second?" Matt says, not looking away from me.

"Sure thing, boss. I'll be out in the hallway." Matt walks up to me. I have mixed emotions when I see him—a blend of anger and happiness that I don't know quite what to do with. I'm not even sure what to say to him, but he saves me the trouble of having to decide.

"Damien is a very persuasive guy, you know?"

"What do you want, Matt?"

"I want to let you know that Damien did a great job to show me that both of us—not just you—are pigheaded, stubborn guys, who always think they're right. Sometimes that leads to a clashing of the minds."

"Yeah." I don't really feel like a heart to heart right now. I want to get my body ready and stay focused, but at the same time I feel comforted by him being around. I've never had a fight where he isn't getting me ready in the back. "So, I have to get ready."

"Look," he says. "I get it. I'm still against this, and I really didn't want to be a part of this whole thing—I thought it was a shit idea, and I kind of still do."

"Is there a 'but' in this Matt, cause your timing is shitty right now."

"But," he says, smiling. "You're like my son, and I've been there for you your entire career. Being a coach isn't just being there when your student is doing what you want, but being there for them unconditionally."

He extends his hand. Matt's a stubborn guy, like he said, but he's a man of honor and integrity. There isn't a fake bone in his body, so when he goes to shake a hand and says all is forgiven, I don't even question it. My hands are gloved, so I tap his fist and we hug it out.

"Awww," Damien jokes. "A Kodak moment between men. This is some deep shit."

"Shut up, asshole."

We all laugh, and then Matt gets serious. "Listen, I have some ideas for how you can beat Jason. You wanna hear, or you want to do what you and Damien decided? I respect your decision either way."

That's all I need to hear. "What I need is Master Splinter to help me beat the Shredder."

"What?" he asks. "Does that mean yes?"

"Dude, after this fight we're gonna have to sit down and watch the first movie—you really need to start catching these references I throw at you. There's more to watch online than fight footage."

"If you say so, champ. If you say so."

Champ. I like the sound of that. Time to make it a reality.

CHAPTER THIRTY-FIVE

LUCAS

35 minutes Later

You never get used to a straight punch to the nose, no matter how crappy of a striker your opponent is. It always stings, no matter what. Lucky for me it's not a clean shot. With my hand out of commission, and the fight starting on the feet, I have to use my footwork and angles to avoid getting knocked out. Not that it's a huge risk with Jason—he used to have another nickname on the amateur circuits, Pillow Hands. Not the name you want when you're trying to be an MMA champion, but he had a reputation for being a crap striker and being a cheat.

What he is really good at, though, is Jiu Jitsu. He's a great grappler, and right now I haven't had to deal with any of that. Master Splinter had a great game plan that's all based around psychology. I guess that's why I gave him the nickname—man's a genius when it comes to fighting. Most people have the stereotype of fighting as purely physical, but about ninety percent of it is mental. We all know how to fight—how to grapple, strike, and use footwork. Few of us understand the mental game as well as Matt—and part of victory at a high level is using an opponent's psychology against him.

I slip a few more jabs. A few connect as I'm moving, and I'm trying to keep my jab in his face to maintain distance. I have a pretty significant reach advantage of five inches on him, and I'm going to use it all to keep him the distance I need him from me. If he gets in past that range he'll try to clinch me and take me down so he can use his Jiu Jitsu. If I keep him too far back I won't connect with my jab. I need him right on the end of my working hand, and I need to mask the fact that I'm not throwing any right hands.

That last part is harder than you'd think—after a while he's going to notice that no right-handed punches are coming at him, so I throw a high right kick to mask it. He blocks right away and we're back to jabbing at each other. He dives for a lazy takedown from too far out and I sprawl out so that he can't get a hold of my legs. I'm happy to let him burn his energy out trying for a takedown that definitely isn't happening. He gives up, and we each get back to the feet.

The round goes on like that, and before I know it the bell rings signaling a third of the fight being over. When I get back to the corner, Matt and Damien look intense.

"Who won that one?" I ask.

"Hard to tell. Could go either way. Not a lot happened."

"I know. I'm trying to get my jab off enough to win me the round. That, plus the failed takedown on his part, might win it for me."

"Maybe," Matt says. "But I don't want two more rounds of that. You leave it up to the judges and weird shit can happen. We don't wanna get there in a championship fight. I need you to step it up to phase two."

Phase two. Matt and I discussed it backstage in the locker room. A three-phase game plan that'll hopefully pay off. Phase one was what I just did—keep him at range, see what he's going to try to do, and counter it. Phase two is me stepping up my offense.

The bell for round two goes off—I meet him in the center and throw a spinning back fist with my left hand. I expected him to duck it, but I hit him square in the face and he stumbles back. I hear my coach yell, "He's hurt!" as Jason stumbles back to the cage. I rush at him, throwing left kicks, left hands, and right elbows as he covers up against the cage. This wasn't the plan, but I'm going with it. I'm not paying attention to the fact that almost none of my strikes are getting through his guard. I start to feel the lactic acid building up, and my arms are feeling heavy. With each punch and elbow my arms feel more and more heavy. I realize that I'm punching myself out, and as soon as I slow my attack he throws a wild haymaker and hits me right on the chin.

I don't feel any pain, just the sensation of falling. For a second, I'm not there—my consciousness gone, but when my body crashes against the canvas it snaps me back into reality. He's standing over me. I go to scoot my hips to the side so I can get up, but he drops his weight on top of me and I have to pull full guard. If you've never had a two hundred and twenty-five-pound man put all of his body weight on you, then you have no idea how crushing it feels. And he knows how to make himself feel even heavier than he is.

I get him into what's called butterfly guard, with the insteps of each of my feet on his upper inner thighs. With that I can control his weight a little bit, and if he's off balance at any point I can lift him up and maybe get out from underneath. But he's never off balance. Not once. We ride the rest of the clock out with him on top, throwing a punch every now and then. When the bell rings I get up and go back to my corner. I don't have to ask who won that one.

"I had that as your round for about forty-five seconds," Matt says.

"Me too. Unfortunately, rounds are five minutes long." You gotta love Damien, he can be a prick even in the most tense of circumstances.

"I'm aware, asshole. So it's 1-1?"

"Probably. We're going to go straight to phase three now. No choice." Phase three. That's where I give him a look he's not expecting. It's do-or-die.

"Alright."

"Listen, Lucas. This is it. This is the last chance you may have. It's now or it's never—so make it now!"

Matt doesn't usually raise his voice—he's more of the measured type, so seeing him get amped up gets me amped up. No matter what happens, I'm going out there to win. The bell sounds, and we meet in the center for a final touch of gloves. Leather hits leather, and then we each step back, ready to do battle.

I take the center first.

I claim my space and keep my hands high in case he tries to knock me out like my last opponent did. He doesn't. He just throws a couple of lazy shots. He's standing low, with a huge bend in his knees, and that only means one thing—he's planning on shooting for my legs and taking me down. He knows that I know this, and what he wants is for me to throw something at him that'll put me off balance and make it easier for him to take me to the ground—something like a high kick. I won't be throwing those, or anything else that's going to make his job easier.

Instead of a high kick, I throw a low kick. It's low and slow, slow enough for him to catch, which is exactly what I want him to do. As he grabs my left leg he goes for the takedown, only I've been working one of my favorite submissions—the guillotine choke. It's the perfect counter for a lazy takedown, which he shoots for. Once his head is beneath my armpit, I wrap his neck with my left hand. As he goes to take me down I let him, and as we fall to the canvas together I slip my right arm underneath his neck also and clasp my hands. We land in my full guard, and I cut an angle so that the guillotine is all but locked in.

I squeeze. I squeeze like all hell. My arms are still a little shot from all those punches before, and a guillotine is a strength move. There's technique to it, but it also requires a lot of strength, and I'm hoping I have enough. I see my corner yelling and jumping.

"Squeeze, Lucas, squeeze!"

I listen. I feel him trying to get out, and trust me he knows how, but I don't think he was expecting any offensive Jiu Jitsu from me. I caught him by surprise just enough to sink in a tight choke that is very hard to get out of. I squeeze some more, waiting to see if he's going to try and muscle his way out, but he doesn't. I feel his body go limp, and I feel the fight drain out of him. I get excited and look up at the ref, who's standing above us, watching closely.

"He's out!" I yell. "Check him."

Guillotines are weird for refs because the guy's face is under my arm, facing the canvas, so refs have to be able to read body language and know when a guy's out. If I hold the choke too long after that I could cause brain damage, so

I hope this ref knows what the hell he's doing. I yell again. "He's fucking out!"

"Stop, stop!" The ref grabs my arm and I hear the bell. The fight's over, and I just won the championship!

The crowd erupts, and I fall to my back in complete exhaustion.

I did it.

I fucking did it!

CHAPTER THIRTY-SIX

MILA

"YES!"

My screams barely make a sound in this crowd. I just watched my man win the light heavyweight championship, and I think I may have destroyed my voice screaming. There are too many people here for him to see or hear me, but that doesn't stop me from freaking out. Holly and Sophie are next to me doing the exact same thing as me, and so is everyone else in the arena.

"YES! YOU'RE THE FUCKING CHAMP! YES!"

I don't recognize myself right now. I'm usually pretty calm, but I know what this means. For 99 percent of these people this is just another fight—almost fifteen minutes of entertainment and nothing else. But I know how much went into this, how much it means, and what Lucas was dealing with behind the scenes to get here.

After a post fight interview and a whole lot of celebration in the cage, I try to catch Lucas as he's walking off to the backstage area. I scream his name, wave, and do whatever I can to catch his attention, but he doesn't see me.

I work my way out of the isle and try to run backstage. A giant man who must be security stops me. He looks like The Mountain from Game of Thrones.

"Excuse me, ma'am, you can't go back there."

"But I know the guy who just won. I need to see him."

"Never heard that one before, ma'am. Sorry. Not happening. If you know him, you can catch up with him after he leaves, but right now..."

Just as he's about to turn me away I hear the commotion. A beer bottle smashes against the arena floor and two guys in the crowd start going at it. I guess the fights in the cage weren't enough. The big security man rushes over to break it up before someone gets hurt, and that's when I make my move. I rush past him, down the corridor that I think leads into the backstage area.

I look around like a crazy person, going from locker room to locker room, until I hear the celebration down the hall. That has to be his. I dart over to the last room at the end of the hallway and rush inside like I belong there. No one notices me, and everyone is gathered around Lucas and the new gold belt that he has strapped around his waist.

At first, I don't want to ruin his moment. We haven't really talked yet. I don't want to take away from all this, so I turn around to sneak back out. That's when I hear his voice. "Mila!" he yells. "Mila, wait!" He rushes over to me and wraps his huge, sweaty arms around me, and that's when I know everything is okay. He squeezes me so hard it almost hurts, but it's the best pain I've ever felt. "I didn't know you were here, why didn't you tell me you were coming?"

"I didn't want to distract you," I tell him. "I saw the whole thing! That was a sick guillotine!"

"You remember!" he says. I've never seen him this

happy. He's smiling ear to ear, covered in sweat and blood, but he's never looked so sexy to me.

"Listen, I. . ."

"Stop," he tells me. "I was an asshole. End of story. I took shit out on you that you didn't deserve, and I'll never do that again. And this wouldn't have been a real victory without you here with me. End of story. I fucking love you."

"What?" I ask, not believing my ears.

"I said I love you, and without you here this strap doesn't mean shit."

"I love you, too," I tell him, jumping into his arms and squeezing as hard as I can.

"Easy, easy killer, I just fought another guy. I'm sore as hell."

"Oh, jeez, sorry."

"How about when all this dies down, we go to dinner and celebrate? Someplace nice."

"Are you sure? You don't want to hang out with the guys?"

"I see the guys enough. I'll see them tomorrow. People are gonna come for this strap. There's plenty of gym time to come, but right now the only person I want to see is you. What do you say?"

"I say yes—to anything you ask me."

He leans into me and puts his mouth next to my ear. "I'll remember you said that later on."

He takes my hand. I stay in the locker room with him until it clears out. He takes a quick shower and gets changed. He looks good dressed up. "Ready?" he asks.

"I'm ready."

As he's grabbing his bags, a man appears in the doorway and calls Lucas' name. "Hey, Ghost."

Lucas turns around. "Holy shit, Sean, I didn't even think you were here tonight."

"I'm always around," he says. "That was an impressive win tonight. Listen, if you have a second, I'd like to talk. I think we have a few things to go over."

Lucas turns to me and smiles. "Baby," he says. "No disrespect, but dinner is going to have to wait!"

I thought it might. I think Lucas just got into the UFC! He's right. Dinner can wait.

The End

CHAPTER THIRTY-SEVEN

COMING DECEMBER, 2019

The Three Kiss Clause

Synopsis

Cormac Delaney was everything I hated about men—arrogant, smug and condescending, but he was also everything my body responded to—gorgeous, tall, brooding, and confident. Oh, and he happened to be a partner at the publishing company I was trying to get signed to! My book —"Fu*#$@Boys"—about how men are selfish, sex-crazed pigs—was one vote of 'yes'—his vote—from being a published, but not only did he hate my book, he asked me a question that would change things between us forever:

"How can you be an expert on men when you've never been in a real relationship?"

He had a point, but I wasn't about to let him know. Instead I did what any self-respecting academic would do—I proposed a radical social experiment. Cormac and I would live together for one month as boyfriend and girlfriend. If he could change my mind about men I'd withdraw my book. If not, he'd agree to publish it.

My only condition? No sex, or anything physical, whatsoever.

I never thought he'd go for it, but I guess I was wrong about him, in more ways than one. Don't get me wrong, I hate Cormac Delaney, even if he is easy on the eyes. . .fine, he's good looking. . .alright, he's hot as hell, but still! To do this I'm going to have to remind myself of a few things: we're only an experiment, nothing more. He's *not* the most gorgeous man I've ever seen in my life, he absolutely *does not* have a body that makes me tingle in all the right places, and I'm *never*, under any circumstances, going to let myself fall for him. . .

Right?

FuckBoy

—Someone who is only looking for a piece of ass to use then throw away. . . He will always come crawling back because he is a horny prick and cannot withstand the dispossession of one of his baes, because he has more than one that's for sure.

FuckBoy Syndrome

—A chronic disease, in which a chemical imbalance located between the testicles and brain cause the affected male to act and think in a distorted and perverted way. No one knows the exact cause of Fuckboy Syndrome, but it is said to be both genetic and conditioned. If this disease is left to manifest, it will consume the fuckboys life and actions.

—Urban Dictionary

CHAPTER ONE

TORI

Let's get one thing straight.

Men are pigs, nothing more—slaves to the masters that are their dicks.

Don't bother arguing with me on this point, because my mind is firmly made up. In fact, I've written a book on that very subject that's (hopefully) soon to be published. I read that you should have an eye-catching title—something that'll grab readers right away, so I've decided to call mine *Fuckboys: A Sociological Analysis of Men's Sexual Habits.* I have a pitch meeting coming up at my dream publishing company tomorrow, and if all goes well, then you'll probably see me at your local Barnes & Noble signing copies —I can't wait to meet you!

But we do need to clear the air on a few things before I sign my (soon to be a bestseller) book for you. I've been called a lot of names because of my (totally justifiable) views on men—*radical feminist,* a *man-hater,* and, of course, people's favorite all-encompassing female insult—a *bitch.* I'm none of those things. I'm just a strong, ambitious, intellectual woman who isn't afraid to tell it like it is. If that offends you, then maybe we won't be seeing each other at your local Barnes & Noble after all.

It's okay—my views aren't for everyone. Like my mom used to say, I'm like Swiss cheese—I'm an acquired taste.

Even my best friend in this world, Jenny, disagrees with me. We were having this debate the yesterday. Actually, we're always having this debate. She's the opposite of me in almost every way—trusting, happy-go-lucky, outgoing, and generally keeps on believing in the inherent goodness of men, no matter how many times she gets screwed over. This is how our conversation went.

"You can't call all men pigs," she told me.

"I don't know how you can disagree with me so hard."

"Probably because I'm not a bitter old lady with a dried-up vagina full of dead spiders and cobwebs."

"Jesus, Jenny, that was really graphic, even for you."

"Well, in my head I was going to call it either a desert or a frozen Siberian tundra—I like contrasts, and I thought as a writer you'd appreciate a good metaphor, but for some reason I pictured spiders and cobwebs."

"I appreciate that. I really, really do, as well as your concern about the state of my vagina. Do you think about it often?"

"Your pussy?"

"Yeah."

"I wouldn't say often—that's a little aggressive. It's kind of like a parent with their kid."

I can't keep a straight face when she talks. I try. I really do. "What? You're going to have to explain that one."

"I don't have any kids of my own—that I know of, anyway—but I imagine it's like when I hear my friends who are moms describe how they're always worried about the safety of their little ones. It's kind of like that."

"So, in that tortured—yet hilarious metaphor, you're my pussy's mom? You're kind of a helicopter mom at that."

"Exactly."

"Well, just so you don't worry, all's good down below. You don't have to worry anymore. And I'm not an old lady."

"Not literally. But inside you're like a bitter divorcee who hates all men."

"I don't hate all men, just so you know, I just. . . have some strong opinions on them. And, to go full circle here, I don't understand how you feel any different. Sure, I don't have much experience in this area, but you do."

"Did you just call me a whore?"

"In a gentle, best friend kind of way. But yeah, kinda."

"I'm okay with it, I was just asking. Go on."

I laugh so hard. "I mean, look at your last four—that's *four*—boyfriends. Shitheads, one and all, each worse than the last."

"You're not wrong. I even have them as 'Ex-Dick #'s 1-4' in my phone now. I don't have the heart to erase their numbers. But yeah, it's true, I've had some bad luck with the XYs."

"Four douche bags in a row isn't bad luck, Jenny, it's evidence of why women need my book. In my qualitative research, I interviewed about twenty women in our age range and they all had the same experiences."

"Bad boyfriends, you mean?"

"That's an understatement. There are levels of bad. You should hear some of the shit they told me about their relationships."

"Oooh, spill the tea—anonymously, of course. I know you can't tell me their names."

225

"I'll give you the blurbs—he cheated on me, he slept with my sister, he gave me two different STDs from all the prostitutes he was sleeping with, he left me after I wouldn't have sex with him four times a week. . . and on and on they went. There was literally not a single one of them who didn't have something bad to say about more than one of their exes."

"And you think that means that all men are like that?"

"No, it doesn't mean that at all, but it definitely means that there's something to what I'm saying. I'm not totally crazy."

"No one's totally crazy, Tor. I mean, maybe like, Charles Manson. He was pretty fucking batshit, but when it comes to someone like you, I'd say you're only like sixty-five percent crazy. That's a good number I think."

"Is it my fault that all my female subjects tell me is how the men in their lives—brothers, friends, boyfriends, husbands, fathers and yes, wait for it—even grandfathers, are running around twenty-four seven trying to stick their little dicks into everything?"

"Don't say that, Tori. That's not fair. Some of them have pretty substantial dicks."

"I'm sure they do. I wouldn't know."

"Wait, how big was. . . he-who-shall-remain-nameless' dick? Like, I know you didn't measure or anything. Unless you did, which would be some kinky shit—but forget that, just give me an approximation? Was it like a pencil—long and thin? Or was it more cucumber-ish?"

"Jenny, stop it. . ."

"Oh, don't tell me he was packing a full eggplant down there?"

"Jenny!"

"Sorry. Sorry. I got carried away with thoughts of. . ."

"I don't want to talk about *him*—ever really, but especially not right now."

The 'him' in question is my ex-boyfriend from college—really the only boyfriend I ever had. It's sad to say, but that experience changed all of my opinions on guys in general. I've basically been as celibate as a Tibetan monk ever since. After college, relationships were like that drink you order on your twenty-first birthday, drink too much of, and then can never smell again without vomiting on the floor.

"I get it. I know he hurt you bad, but. . ."

"Jenny, I really don't want to . . ."

"I know, just let me finish. I'm pulling the bestie card. That's a thing. I know that whole thing back in school. . . didn't go the way you thought it would, but welcome to the club."

"That's my whole point!"

"No, you're missing the point. What I'm saying is that yes, every woman has some horror story of some guy—or even multiple guys in their lives. But we don't all become as bitter as you are. I will never understand how you got so jaded at the ripe old age of twenty-eight. How can you hate men so much?"

"Let's be clear," I told her. "I don't hate men. My brother is a man, and I love him as much as anyone. My doctoral advisor is a man, and he's like a father to me. My actual father is everything to me. I don't hate men, I just see them for what they are. There's a difference."

"And what are they?"

"Penises attached to arms, legs, and the occasional semi-functioning brain. They're all a walking hard on, Jenny, and just about all of their behaviors are geared towards one activity and one activity only—screwing as many women as they can before the sun sets. Then they go to sleep, to rest up, so they can get their fuck energy back for the next day's hunt. They're like sexual nomads, wandering the vast plains of America looking for willing vaginas."

"Wow. You're messed up, Tori."

"Why am I messed up?" I asked. "Because I speak the truth all women already know but are afraid to admit?"

"First reason is because you came up with the phrase 'fuck energy' off the top of your head. Second, because there have to be guys out there that aren't what you're describing. You just haven't interviewed the women who know those guys. Or you only asked them about bad experiences, so those are the stories they told you. Doesn't that have a name, like in science?"

"Selection bias," I told her, angry that she knows terms that can prove me wrong. "That's called selection bias."

"Well, there you go. You selected wrong. Or at least you selected. . . selectively. You know what I'm saying. I hate all that science stuff."

She was right, of course, and I know not ALL men are piggish fuckboys, but I haven't met or heard of ones who aren't. There has to be something to that.

"I know that not every single human with a penis and an XY chromosome set exists solely to fuck and screw women over. Just like I know some people in prison are wrongfully convicted, but most aren't."

"I think this is the point in the conversation where I need to reintroduce my suggestion that you see a therapist."

"I told you the first time—and just about every time after that—I don't need therapy just 'cause men are sex crazed pigs. It isn't me that needs to change. I'm just holding up a mirror to an entire gender, don't blame the reflection." Jenny tells me I need therapy at least once a month, usually when I'm on an epic rant about men, or discussing my work

—which is largely the academic version of ranting about men.

"I disagree," she told me for the umpteenth time. "But whatever, do you. I still want you to get that book deal—partially because I love you—like ninety perfect that, but also, I really want to appear in the acknowledgments of a book sometime in my life. So yeah, good luck tomorrow."

"Awww," I said really sarcastically. "You're so sweet."

"I have my moments. Just consider my point of view. I'm a woman too, you know? I have a vagina just like you, only mine is alive and well."

"I'm sure it is."

She sat up really straight at that point, like a lightbulb had just gone off in her crazy little head. "Wait, maybe that's it! I never thought of it before."

"Though of what?" I asked.

"Why, of all the male behaviors you like to focus on, do you have an obsession with thinking men want sex at all times? But not all male behavior is geared towards sex."

"You're right," I told her. "Most is. The rest is reserved for the subjugation of women."

"Oh my God, Tori, you need to have an orgasm right now. What did you do with the vibrator I got you?"

"Jesus, lower your voice."

We were getting lunch—some vegan place that Jenny found right after her conversion to all things non-living. She was flaky like that. I gave her veganism about as long as I gave her when she texted me telling me that she met 'the perfect guy'—about two to four weeks, max. Knowing her, our next lunch would probably be at a steakhouse, which was just fine with me. The place we had this conversation was one of those spots that was super judgy towards us meat-eating folk, yet they also tried desperately to court a meat-eating clientele by having fake meat dishes, promising that they tasked like, and I quote, 'the real thing.' They did not.

"What, now you're embarrassed?" she asked, taking a bite of her sweet potato. . . something or other. "You didn't care if anyone heard you declaring the inherent evil of the entire male species, but I mention touching yourself and you get all. . ."

"Shhh!"

"Oh, wow," Jenny said. It was judgmental. It was something I'd do. I did not appreciate it. I can't take my own medicine. I can't take just as good as I give. "I just figured you out. Like, a lightbulb just went off. Can you see it?"

I look over her head and we both laugh. "Nope. Strangely, I can't."

"Don't worry, it's there, whether you see it or not. It's glowing just as bright, regardless."

"That's good to know," I joked. "And what is said lightbulb illuminating for you?"

"Something I should have realized years ago. It's so simple. You're afraid of sex."

Leave it to her to bring it right back to that. "What? You're nuts."

"Interesting that you bring up nuts, firstly. And secondly, I think I'm onto something here. Let's examine the evidence, shall we Dr. Tori Klein?"

"Well, there's no evidence to explore, so we really can't do that, can we?"

"Hear me out. You're obsessed with men having sex. Or, at least with them *trying* to have sex all the time, like it's some global conspiracy to keep women down. So, you see men wanting sex as threatening, and you're uncomfortable talking about masturbation or orgasms."

I hate that Jenny has an undergrad degree in psychology. You know what they say about having a little knowledge about something—well, that's her when it comes to anything psychological. She remembers a few lectures from college and tries to use them to 'diagnose' me with whatever she thinks is wrong.

"I don't like talking about getting myself off in public— that doesn't make me a prude, it just makes me someone with standards."

"Don't get all high and mighty like you like to do, Tori. It's not like I whipped out the little bean tickler right here at the table."

I started giggling. "Excuse me? The bean tickler?"

"Yeah," she said. "You know? The joystick. The pussy pleaser."

"Oh my God, how are we friends?"

"Wait, I wasn't done. The hole pole, Happy Feelmore, BOB."

"Excuse me, BOB?"

"Yeah, Battery-Operated-Boyfriend. BOB. We all know BOB—some of us know him a little better than others. BOB's not a bad guy—he's there to help bring us to a higher plane of existence. We love BOB. We need him in our lives."

I started cracking up then, and so did Jenny. "Look, I'm not scared of sex. And I'm not an old lady with a cobweb vagina."

"Actually, I said that you had cobwebs *in* your vagina, but whatever."

"Well, I'm not that. . . I'm just. . . guarded when it comes to that kind of stuff. He-who-shall-not-be-mentioned took care of that for me. Now I spend so much time giving men shit for their sex lives that I don't really have much of a chance to have my own. I mean, what guy would even try to approach me? I scare them away, and I have really high standards. It would take a lot for me to even feel something towards a man like that."

"Look, all I'm saying is that it's possible to separate the two," she told me. "You can have your selection bias ridden research, telling you how men are the worst people in the world for getting all of those pesky erections, and you can also still be normal in your personal life—still be a woman without feeling guilty about it. It's okay to like men, to want them, to have those feelings. That doesn't invalidate your book. What invalidates it is that you don't ever actually put yourself out there and try—you're commentating from the bench. You need to get in the game."

When Jenny speaks like she did at lunch yesterday, I always want to believe what she's saying to me, but I can never seem to get there. It's like I have this shield around me when it comes to guys. I know where that shield comes from, but I can't get rid of it. On top of that, every time I talk to another woman about their experiences, all of my feelings on men come right back to the forefront of my mind.

I look down at the worn-out copy of my book that I had printed. I hope tomorrow goes well, because all I've ever wanted was to be a published author.

I have to admit, this is easily the best thing I've ever written!

CHAPTER TWO

CORMAC

The Following Afternoon

"This is total bull crap!"

God, I shouldn't have said that out loud, should I? Probably not the most appropriate thing for a partner in a huge publishing company to say to an aspiring author. Even if she is as much of a social justice feminist nut as this Dr. Tori Klein seems to be. Seriously, I've never read such crap in my entire life, and I read books for a living! I look back down at the text just in case I'm being unfair. Nope. Nope, I'm not.

Toxic masculinity?
Manspreading?
Mansplaining?

Who made up all of these stupid terms? I look over and see one of my partners, Elissa, smiling and nodding so hard that her neck must be getting sore. Am I in the *Twilight Zone*? Am I the only one with any sense?

"Cormac!" Elissa shouts. "Don't be rude. Tori is in the middle of her pitch."

Tori Klein.

Excuse me, *Dr.* Tori Klein. I know these academic types get their panties in a bunch if you don't use the pretentious titles they spend a lifetime in school to earn.

I read up on her. I like to do my research before authors come to sit down and pitch an idea, it gives me a better sense of what to expect when they're sitting across from me. This one's a recent Ph.D. in Sociology. She describes herself as a, and I quote, *liberal third wave feminist* (I didn't know they came in waves, but whatever), and apparently, she's some kind of hot shot in the academic world. It said online that she's the youngest woman to ever be offered a tenure track position at the University. Her dissertation—which this shit book she's pitching is based on—won a bunch of awards. Blah, blah, blah.

As far as I'm concerned, the only thing this girl has going for her is her face and body, because lord knows her work is progressive trash. But back to that face and body—both are ridiculous. I can't hate on her looks, no matter what I think of her professional work. She's not just the hottest woman to ever pitch a book in this office, she's one of the most gorgeous women I've ever seen. It's getting harder and harder. . . to concentrate, that is.

I read up one some of her academic papers and blog posts. It was total feminist bull crap. If it were just up to me, I'd never have even let her in the door—not when there are real authors a mile long trying to publish real content with us. But I have partners—two of them, both women—and they both loved the sample chapters that the annoyingly hot Dr. Tori Klein provided to us.

I guess I should go back to listening to whatever drivel she's rattling on about. Our publishing company has an agreed upon policy of 'unanimous or no' – meaning that we all have to agree that we're going to accept a book for publication, or the book gets rejected. Every one of us has veto power, and based on the silly, happy grin on Elissa's face, I think I'm going to be using mine very soon.

"Tori, please keep going."

"No, Tori," I say, interrupting before this goes any further. "Please stop."

"Cormac!"

"Elissa, I love you, but you're off here. You're telling me that I need to be polite in a meeting where I have to listen to this. . . scholar. . . tell me how awful men are? Doesn't that seem a little contradictory to you?"

The only reason I'm even still sitting at this table is because of how sexy this woman is. She's bat-shit crazy with this book she thinks I'm going to publish, but with a face and body like that I'm almost ready to forgive her. Almost. She jumps in to defend herself. "Mr. . ."

"Cormac is fine," I tell her. "Or should I call myself. . . hold on, let me find it." I page back through her last chapter until I find what I'm looking for. "Ah, maybe I should call myself a '...cis man patriarch.' But I guess that is a little too wordy to say, huh? Doesn't really roll off the tongue, does it?"

Tongue. I wonder what hers would feel like in my mouth. Fuck, Cormac, focus!

My partner jumps in to do what she always thinks she needs to do—apologize for me and make excuses for my behavior. She thinks I'm rude. I think I'm honest. "Tori, I'm so sorry. He's just a very blunt person."

"Now Elissa, don't go mansplaining away my behavior." I use the most mocking tone I can, going out of my way to confirm all of her stereotypes. "Did I use that right? There are so many derogatory terms beginning with the prefix 'man', it's hard to keep them all straight. You'd think these radical feminists would be more creative with their made-up terminology."

"Cormac!" Elissa yells.

The author puts her hand up like the Fascist she seems to be. Mussolini would have been proud. "I've got this one, Elissa." She turns to me, and gives me a look like she enjoys a little back and forth. I'm happy to accommodate. "You think a woman having all these beliefs makes her a radical? So, any woman who has a strong point of view is a radical to you?"

"No, Tori. I think any woman who has radical points of view is a radical. Any book that makes claims about all men is no different than a book that would attempt to make a claim about an entire race or an entire religion—it's discriminatory and promotes generalizations. It's, you know, *radical*."

"You're right, Cormac. The world is hard for upper class white men these days, isn't it? What, with all the rights minorities and woman have."

Oh. Shit. The gloves just came off. I thought she wanted to spar a few rounds, but what she really wants to do is have herself an old-school fight. "I'd expect a better argument from someone as renowned as you than just a simple deflection."

"Deflection?" she asks.

"That's right. I just told you that I think any book that espouses to know what all men are like has, by definition, a bigoted point of view, and that's not the kind of work I want published here."

"Is that how you choose your authors, Cormac? Those who agree with political points of view get deals and you insult everyone else?"

The balls on her. I hold the fate of her publishing future in my hands right now. You'd think she'd be kissing my ass and thanking me for my critical feedback, but instead she's self-sabotaging just to try to win a fight with me. I should stop the meeting right here, thank her for her time, and tell her that she'd do better shopping her book elsewhere, but I don't. I engage instead, because I'm stubborn like that.

"Not at all, Tori. I don't need the books published here to agree with all of my opinions. I just need them to not be baseless and crazy. So far your work is both."

"Baseless and crazy? I can assure you it's neither."

Her cheeks are getting flushed. She's sexy when she's angry. "Okay then. You're an academic, right?"

"Yes," she answers.

"And academics use the scientific method to approach research, correct? They use evidence to back up their claims?"

"Of course."

"So, where exactly is the evidence that anything you're saying in this book is true? I mean. . ." I look back on the opening page of her first chapter. "Your basic premise, if I'm reading you correctly is that, and I quote, 'Men are, by their very nature, selfish and base creatures. This condition comes from a combination of nature and nurture, but is nonetheless a true statement of men's nature.' Now, where's the rest? Here we go—quoting you again, 'Due to this condition, relationships benefit men more than they do women, who end up providing for what their male partner needs without any return.' That's a pretty crazy claim, Doctor. So, I'll reiterate. What's your evidence?"

"Excuse me?" she says with a smug tone. "My evidence?"

"Yes, your evidence. Where do you get your research

from? What makes any of these claims about men generalizable—or even true?"

"I can assure you, Cormac, this book was well researched. If my methodology was good enough for my dissertation committee, it should be good enough for you."

This chick is so full of herself. "I see. Well, unfortunately for you this meeting doesn't end with a new degree. You need to convince us—convince me—so, for the third time, what kind of research is this book based on?"

"I read a lot feminist literature, and did a lot of qualitative interviews with women about their relationship experiences."

"So, you read other books by women like you, who also have no evidence, and then you use them as your evidence. Makes sense."

That's all Elissa wants to hear. She jumps in finally. "Okay, that's enough from both of you. This isn't a productive meeting for anyone right now."

I put my hand up. Not to be dismissive of my partner, but just to get my last point in. I'm a partner, after all, and I have the right to vet any authors we sign in any way I want. But I see the two of them looking at each other when I put my hand in the air in some kind of female solidarity—like, *there he goes, being all male again, trying to control us.* Elissa has taken a big old gulp of the Kool-Aid.

"I just have one more question, if you'll indulge me, Ms. Klein."

"Dr. Klein."

"My apologies. If you'll indulge me, Tori, I just have one last question."

"Yes?"

"It states in your introduction that, despite the fact that you're writing as a scholar of male and female relationships, that you've never been in a serious, long term one yourself. Is that correct?"

She takes a big deep breath, as though I'm the asshole for asking what should be an obvious, critical question. "Yes. It says it right there."

"And why did you put that in there?"

"As an academic, you always have to be prepared for how people will attack and criticize your work. There's no one who knows the limitations and weaknesses of their own material better than someone in my world. So, I put that out there just to get in front of it."

"But, it's a true statement?"

"Yes, it's true."

"Why haven't you been in a serious relationship before?" I ask.

"I don't see how that's any of your. . ."

"My business?" I ask. "Actually, that's exactly what it is —this is *my business*, and you want me to publish a book that'll have my name on the inside flap and back cover. There's a reason I'm asking. How can you claim to know all about men and relationships if you've never actually experienced one yourself? Leaving all of your so-called research coming from feminist theory and academic research?" I let that one hang in the air. I think it's a perfectly valid question, but Elissa seems to think otherwise.

"Cormac, you're way out of line now. This meeting is over, and don't you dare put your hand up to me again. The Q & A portion is finished. Thank you for coming in, Tori. This is groundbreaking and very appropriate work for the modern political climate that we find ourselves in these days."

I stand up. I can't take it anymore. "You're right, this *is* over, and I've heard enough. I say no. I'm sorry, but this isn't for us." I throw down a copy of her manuscript on the desk, still open to the page that tells me what a horrible misogynistic prick I am. Oh, wait, that's every page. I walk out of the hostile room and head into my office. I have some real books to read.

Before I'm completely out of the room I steal one more look at her.

She really is so beautiful.

It's a damn shame she hates men so much.

My Newsletter Sign up—> http://eepurl.com/cg0vav

BookBub—> https://www.bookbub.com/authors/
christopher-harlan

Goodreads—>   https://www.goodreads.com/author/
show/15894914.Christopher_Harlan

Amazon—> https://www.amazon.com/-
/e/B01M1KU74Y

Instagram—>www.
instagram.com/authorchristopherharlan

BOOKS BY CHRISTOPHER HARLAN

Away From Here: a young adult novel

Synopsis:

When I was seventeen years old there were only three things that I knew for certain: I was a mixed up mixed kid, with weird hair and an unhealthy love of comics; I wanted to forget I'd ever heard the words depression and anxiety; and I was hopelessly in love with a girl named Annalise who was, in every way that you can be, a goddess. What can I say about Anna? She wasn't the prom queen or the perfect girl from the movies, she was my weird, funny, messed up goddess. The girl of my dreams. The reason I'm writing these words.

I'd loved Anna from a distance my junior year, afraid to actually talk to her, but then one day during lunch my best friend threw a french fry at my face and changed everything. The rest, as they say, is history. Our History. Our Story. Annalise helped make me the man I am today, and loving her saved my teenaged soul from drowning in the depths of a terrible Bleh, the worst kind of sadness that there is, a concept Anna taught me about a long time ago, when we were younger than young. So flip the book over, open up the cover and let me tell you Our Story, which is like Annalise, herself - complicated, beautiful, funny, and guaranteed to teach you something by the time you're through. Maybe it'll teach you the complexity of the word potato, something I never understood until the very last page.

Our Story: an Away From Here Prequel (Amazon FREE download)—> http://a.co/fYScly5

#1 bestseller—*Away From Here: A Young Adult Novel*
Amazon —> http://a.co/di866wQ
Goodreads (4.61/5 stars)—> https://www.
goodreads.com/book/show/38212508-away-from-here

This duet follows the interrelated stories of two best friends, Mia and Dacia, as they encounter the Marsden brothers—two mysterious, handsome, and intriguing men whose family has a sordid history that they must discover together:

Impressions of You (book 1)—> http://a.co/786mkFA

Impression of Me (book 2)—> http://a.co/4MI4gw3

THE NEW YORK CITY'S FINEST

HEA contemporary romance—My 5 book series, a blend of contemporary romance, action, suspense, and adventure—each book features a different sexy NYPD detective and takes place in a different borough of New York. Follow these NYPD detectives as they meet the women of their dreams while trying to solve the crimes of their careers!

Calem (book 1)—> http://a.co/hEyPn3Q

Jesse (book 2)—> http://a.co/eyTkL7I
Quinn (book 3)—> http://a.co/gO9YJ7m
Noah (book 4)—> http://a.co/2xvrb7p
Riley (book 5)—>http://a.co/5YRvjxv

Or, you can get all of the books bundled:

The New York City's Finest Boxed Set (all 5 books)
—> http://a.co/1D3kw4i

THE WORDSMITH CHRONICLES

HEA contemporary romance—A group of aspiring romance writers struggle with trying to make it big in the indie publishing world while navigating their love lives.

Knight (book 1)—> http://a.co/iBcVaK5
Colton (book 2)—> http://a.co/dy2Ojmq
Grayson (book 3)—> http://a.co/d/43MNyLS

True North: A Wordsmith Chronicles Standalone MC—> http://a.co/d/iSlpvVo
North: A Wordsmith Chronicles Standalone—>
My Book

STANDALONE HEA CONTEMPORARY ROMANCE

Standalone HEA Contemporary Romance:

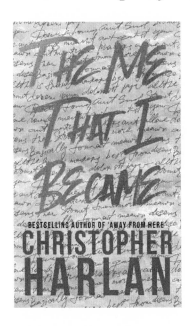

The Me That I Became

Synopsis:

We were destined to never end up together. You an empath, and me the woman who can't feel anything. It never should have worked.Then our hands brushed together. It was serendipity—a happy accident that made me experience the world like I never had before. You said all the right words, and for a time I remembered what it felt like to be alive.But my shadows have returned, threatening to extinguish the light you brought into my life, and I'm terrified that our future together is slipping away. I need you now, Brandon. I need you to chase away the demons, to make me whole, and to teach me once again what it means to love. Now only one question remains. . .Will you?

Amazon—> http://a.co/d/orjzTBu
Goodreads—> https://www.goodreads.com/book/show/42551351-the-me-that-i-became

THE SICK PARENTS CLUB: A NOVEL

Synopsis

"The bullet let loose on July 22nd, 1939, destroyed a house full of children who went to sleep normal, but awoke forever deformed. The bullet ricocheted, lodging itself so deep inside each of them that none realized they'd been hit until years

later. There were no survivors that day, even though there were many."

So begins the latest work from bestselling novelist Nathan Dunbar, as he chronicles the dark secret that forever altered the trajectory of his family. As he struggles to complete that book, he realizes that another story begs to be written—the story of his own teenaged years, a time he spent asking questions about the origin of his parent's mental illnesses, and forging a bond with the best friends he's ever know.

As he writes memories flood back—of summer days spent playing basketball, of surviving his household with his twin sister, Clover, and the way he felt when Serafina moved in to the neighborhood. That summer he experienced something he only told her, something he's never allowed himself to express until now, and when he does it will force a confrontation between the future he wants and the past he struggles to reconcile with.

Welcome to the Sick Parents Club.

Amazon—> My Book
Goodreads—>https://www.goodreads.com/book/show/4407647 1-the-sick-parents-club

ACKNOWLEDGMENTS

To all the readers who helped support this book through their shares, comments, likes, and overall support—this wouldn't be possible without you. And, specifically: Donna Tanner, Tiffany Diamond, KarriLu Brown, Sue Kelly Rugolo, Rebecca Katrina Williams, Laura Shelnutt, Deana Renfroe, Jodi Riley, Becky Dietrich, Stephanie Lashbrook, Vicki Urwin Briers, Stephanie Puterbaugh, Carol Thomas, Valerie Perkins Savage, Rosie Cruz, Winter Jensen, Jennifer Albert, Audrey Lei Lacambra, Jennifer Lovins, Maria Esther Jiron, Brittany Whitmire, Vickie Beams, Ann Zimmer, Kimberly Field, Ana Perez, Shannon Botkin, Rochelle West, Carol LillianRhaine Mills, Jaime Deihmann, Tiffany Brocato, Bonnie Bracken, Elizabeth Gray, Valerie Clarkson, Nelida Rodriguez, Chelsea Hackert, Andrea Flatness Kollmer, Dani Kendrick, AnnaMarie Hay, Suzanne Stanley, Deb Meade Cechak, Melanie Stevenson, Shirley Werner, Heather Swan, Tricia Read, Krystal K. Gaston, Rachel Miller, Laura Anderson, Amy Jenkins, Wendy Johnson-Hamm, Tristian Lyn Klein, Shelley Peake, Shelly Reynolds, Cat Wright, Jennifer

Marie, Jill Blackwell, Dawn Barrett Connolly, Chris Finizio, Jessica Wade, Joni Foster, Monica Cruz, Geri Lambre Nelson, Mindy Herbert, Virginia Swanson, Colleen Quirk, Cheryl Johnson, Jess Jug, Jackie Ortiz, Lauren Mitchell, Meghan Depp, Amber Marie Brazell, Katie Reads, Anna Sweets, Bookluvin Rose, Crystal Matz-Waldele PA, Pam Nicholson, Jenn Campos, Ches Daniele, Latochia Hawkins, Lisa Vital Pena, Catherine Weir, Chris Cox, Cynthia Krietz, Tabitha Totten, Mary Luke Young, Amanda O'Brien, Sharon Baum, Michaela Zankl, Deb Anderson Sisler, Theresa Pierce, Jennifer Rusher Minton, Amanda Barron, Amber Tillman, Emma Toole, Vicky Langley Kimble, Ellen Farrelly, Brenda Buschmann, Tina Meyers, Raven Johnson, Jamie Margulis Speck, Tammy Lynn, Sandra Foy, Brandy Freed, Linda Rimer-Como, Christina Burrus, Heather Trudeau, Danielle Kodiak, JoAnn Todero, Race Crespin, Lg Reads, Misty Campbell, Chelle Underwood, Terri Dixon, Brenda Parsons, Shannon White, Cindy Hughes, Melissa Livaditis, Kerri Miller, Desiree Ann Hill Leonard, Rebecca K. Kleckner, Lisa Hemming, Denise Rand Huebner, Jessica Laws, Terren Hoeksema, Brenda Pratt, Nicole Minney, Kandi Tomlinson, Tina Laurelli, Samantha Simms, Lee Shaw, Raelene Moore Smith, Maria Rivera, Pamela Sims, Debbie Eichler, Heather Rollins Himmelspach, Claire Jenni Alexander, Penny Fetchen, Maggie Martin, Heather Evers, Angelina Smith, Sexy Books & Sarcasm, Ramblings From SEKS, Jamie Kocurek, Weekly Reads, Dearly Loved m/f books, Erin Reads A Lot, Brooke Gingerella, Tina Meyers, Book Lovers Pit Stop, More Books Please, Shirley's Bookshelf, Becky's Bookshelf, Rabid Readers Book Blog,